Nightmare's Edge

Where the lines between realities and nightmares become blurred.

by William Blackwell

NIGHTMARE'S EDGE

First edition. December 4, 2012.

Copyright © 2012 William Blackwell.

ISBN: 978-1738971435

Written by William Blackwell.

Life is not a journey to the grave with the intention of arriving safely in a pretty and well-preserved body, but rather to skid in broadside, thoroughly used up, totally worn out, and loudly proclaiming, "Wow-what a ride!"
—Gary Swenson

To Gwen, for exorcising my demons.

Chapter One

6:54 pm, Thursday, December 15th, Puerto Plata, Dominican Republic.

Nels Watson honked the horn at a motorcycle that suddenly cut him off. The driver ignored the gesture and slammed on his brakes to avoid a boy who was running across the road, oblivious to the bustling traffic on a busy street in Puerto Plata. Nels slammed on the brakes to avoid hitting both the motorcycle and the little boy.

The boy stumbled, fell, picked himself up and darted to the curb, narrowly avoiding becoming road kill.

No sense flipping him the bird. This is just what it's like in parts of the Dominican Republic. Total mayhem on the roads and people seem used to it. In fact, they seem to thrive on it, going about their business as calmly as possible with horns blasting, vehicles cutting each other off, pedestrians jockeying for position, and noise pollution the likes of which could drive a first-world citizen out of their mind.

But you got used to it. And Nels was used to it as he had navigated these streets before in a rental car and after a week he was as bad, if not worse, than the locals.

The light turned green and vehicles converged from all directions. Nels inched forward. *What's wrong? The light must be broken.* The motorcycle in front of him roared to a start, blowing a thick cloud of black smoke into the windshield of his black four-door sedan. *Shit, this is crazy even by Dominican standards*, he thought as horns blasted him from all directions while attempting to clear the intersection.

"Focus," he said out loud, checking the GPS unit for directions.

"Shit, this thing doesn't seem to be working," he said to no one in particular. He pressed the "where to" button on the GPS as he turned onto a busy side street, trying to buy time to figure out where he was going.

Where am I going?

Then he remembered. He was going to an apartment building in Puerto Plata to visit some friends. That's right, they were waiting for him.

A couple of loud honks on a horn blasted him out of his reverie. He found a space that looked like a parking stall and pulled in, waking a mangy sleeping dog that yelped and scampered. He fidgeted with the GPS but it still would not lock in his position. It kept saying "acquiring satellite."

Nels stared at the unit, hoping it would lock in a signal. He was geographically challenged at the best of times and he didn't consider this the best of times. The hot afternoon sun was giving way to dusk and the streets of Puerto Plata could be extremely dangerous at night. *Relax, you have a car. Just try and remember where the building is.*

"Turn right in five hundred meters," the sexy English voice on the GPS said. *Great. It locked in a signal.* Nels shoulder-checked, then swerved out of the temporary stall, just as an elderly shopkeeper came out, angrily waving a broom at him.

He followed the coordinates to a black low-rise apartment building in a seedy area on the hill with a view of the Atlantic Ocean. Dogs barked, people sang and drank in the streets; a few old men sat at on chairs at a kitchen table on a sidewalk and played dominoes. The streets were strewn with garbage and a few nasty looking characters cast him menacing glances as he passed. This wasn't an upscale area

Sure hope the GPS doesn't fail on the way outta here, Nels thought, knowing if it did he would have a hell of a time getting back to his apartment. *Where am I staying anyway?*

He parked, locked the vehicle, walked into a side entrance and up the stairs to the fourth floor. *Funny, the door should be wide open in a neighborhood like this?*

He knocked on the door a few times and listened. He heard a woman and a man arguing loudly. *Who are they? Right, they're my friends, Belinda and Simon. I've known them for years. I'm sure it's just a minor spat.*

He opened the door and walked in. The room was dimly lit, but for a few candles strategically placed in the corners of the room. Belinda jumped off the couch and smiled at him.

"How are you Nels," she asked, giving him a hug. Simon's agitated demeanor changed and he also smiled.

"Sorry about the noise Nels," Simon said. "You know how it goes. Life wouldn't be any fun if you didn't have the odd spat now and again."

Nels had detected some friction in the relationship a few days back, or was it weeks, he didn't remember now, but he didn't realize it was this bad. This sounded like something that could have erupted into a knock-down, drag-out brawl if he hadn't walked in the door.

"No problem," he said, walking into the kitchen to fix a drink. That's how it was with Belinda and Simon. When they visited Nels, they helped themselves. When he visited them, it was the same story. It's just how close they were.

As Nels poured himself a stiff Cuba libre. He heard his friend's voices become louder. And they didn't sound that friendly. *Should I walk into the room? I suppose I should. They're my friends after all.*

Nels walked into the living room of their two-bedroom flat and looked around. It was sparsely furnished and the TV was turned on. Some HBO movie played in Spanish. He understood the words but didn't get the movie.

They sat together watching the screen and did not acknowledge his entrance. He picked an armchair and sat down.

"What are you watching?" he asked. Belinda glared at him and looked at Simon disgustedly.

What the fuck's going on here? Nels thought. *These two are usually pretty harmonious together.*

Belinda drank a gin and tonic, Simon, a Presidente beer. Nels alternated between rum and fruit juice, rum and water, rum and coke and Bohemia beer on his visits to the DR. He had switched to Bohemia after the price had increased on Presidente.

He still didn't understand what was going on. They both stared at the screen as the image of a vampire biting into its victim played itself out. The male victim screamed and became limp; the sexy female vampire backed away satisfied and smiled at the camera, blood dripping down her mouth, large fangs exposed.

"I don't know what the fuck you thought you were doing but you did it all wrong," Simon said quietly, his features darkening.

Belinda, who was fixated on the horror movie, suddenly jerked her head in Simon's direction.

"Do you even know what you're talking about?" she asked.

It's time for me to leave, Nels thought. He stood, polished off his drink and walked quietly to the door.

The couple glared at each other angrily.

"Look you guys, it's been a slice and thanks for inviting me, but I'm leaving."

Belinda tried to protest, but Nels was already out the door and walking down the stairs. He had never seen his friends so stressed out and confrontational and it worried him. He heard them yelling at each other as he walked down the narrow pathway dotted with palm trees to the street. He glanced at the pool, quiet and blue, on his way out.

Nervously, he jumped into his car and started it. It roared into life on the first turn of the ignition. *I hope the GPS works* was the only thought going through his mind as he shoulder-checked, squealed the tires, and pulled away.

Chapter Two

7:55pm, Thursday, December 15, Puerto Plata.

The streets were dark and unusually quiet as he drove. *Where am I going? Where do I live?* Nels did not have the answers so he tapped the GPS, hoping that it did.

"Acquiring satellite" was all he could read.

He approached a winding corner in the road and realized he was going much too fast to navigate it. He jerked the wheel, trying to bring the black car in line with his course.

It was too little too late.

The car skidded, swerved and crashed into a concrete divide. The momentum of the speed, must have been sixty or seventy miles per hour, sent it soaring airborne. It bounced a few times, finally skidding to a landing upside down, the roof grating along the concrete, sparks flying.

Nels gripped the wheel and wondered when it would end and when he would end.

All was silent.

And black.

He felt his extremities. They were all there. He did not see any blood and he didn't feel any pain. He scraped himself out of the smoking wreckage and looked around.

He was on a street he could not recognize. The buildings were decrepit. He heard dogs barking and loud *merengue* music playing. Not unusual for the DR.

Get a grip.

He felt for his money. It was there. Nels didn't carry a wallet. He never had. He figured if you carry a wallet you make yourself a target in a third world country. And Nels wasn't about to do that. He considered himself a seasoned traveler and he didn't invite problems when he travelled. In fact, he was one of the few people he knew who travelled with only a carry-on bag regardless of the duration of his stay -and on this trip he planned to be here at least three months.

Less is more was his philosophy when travelling. The quicker you can move the safer you are. Anything you need, you can buy. Anything you can't take with you when you leave, you can give away to the poor.

With those thoughts in mind he breathed a sigh of relief as he reached into the smoking vehicle and pulled out his small green knapsack, something most other travelers would view as a day pack, a beach bag large enough for only a few towels, a swimsuit, a few beers and maybe some mosquito repellent and suntan lotion.

But for Nels it was his whole life.

That small nylon green bag he hauled out of the black car that was about to burst into flames represented everything he would need during his stay.

To pack light was an art form. To load up three or four suitcases ... well anybody could do that.

He ran from the vehicle. Half a block away, he looked back. It exploded with a whooshing sound, followed by a big bang. Red flames and black smoke swirled into the black sky.

Fuck, he thought. *Things are going from bad to worse. Where the fuck am I and where do I need to be?* He searched his mind but found no answers.

He carried on down the dark street.

He heard a rustling sound in the hedges immediately in front of him and froze. A black man with freaky large eyes and a freakier afro jumped out of the bush, blocking his path down the narrow sidewalk.

He turned and ran.

"Wait, wait," the black man said.

Nels stopped suddenly and looked behind.

The black man smiled. "I'm here to help you. Follow me."

Without a clear direction, Nels followed the man. He was led to a busy street, the main drag in Puerto Plata, he guessed, and into a small food shack. They sat down together and the man served up rice, beans and chicken, a Dominican staple. Nels looked at the food but didn't have an appetite.

He still didn't know how to get to his apartment. He stepped outside the food shack while the man ate.

Three friends walked by. Nels was excited to see them, thinking they would drive him to his apartment, give him his bearings. They were female, attractive. But all they did was say hello, engage in some perfunctory and mindless chit chat and walk away.

Fuck sakes. Why did they leave? Why would they abandon me? Don't worry, you've got money. And as Nels thought about it, he realized it was just too crazy to be real.

You're in a fucking dream and wake up. But he wasn't waking up. He pinched his arm as hard as he could. Hurt like hell but he still didn't wake up. *Fuck, this isn't a dream. That sucks.*

So he reached into his back pocket for the plastic insurance folder with his money and credit cards. He pulled it out, flipped it open.

Other than a few tattered business cards, it was empty. Not a single credit card. Not a single dollar.

He was broke, lost, confused and horrified.

Wake up, it's a dream. But he couldn't wake up. And it wasn't a dream.

So he stood on a street corner in Puerto Plata, the noise pollution confusing him, blurring the lines between reality and what he thought was a nightmare.

Chapter Three

3:36 am, Thursday, December 15th, Calgary, Alberta, Canada.

His eyes opened and he slowly realized he was in familiar surroundings. His bed, his deep green room, his 50's bungalow. Everything was normal. He looked at his alarm clock.

3:37am.

But his heart raced. Nels had had nightmares for many years and had finally come to embrace them. It was either that or be haunted by them, which he chose not to do.

But this one left a bitter taste in his mouth and he got up, walked into his bathroom and splashed some water on his face. As he looked in the mirror—he saw his eyes bulged in their sockets, his pupils dilated. The image horrified him so he turned away and walked into the kitchen.

He opened the fridge, poured himself a glass of cold water and drained it. His throat felt parched. He hadn't had a cigarette in three months but he walked into the garage and lit up immediately.

Thank god I kept some around for an emergency. He took a long pull on the smoke and exhaled slowly, his heart rate beginning to slow.

What the fuck just happened?

Then he remembered. He searched the calendar hanging on the wall of the man cave for a date. *Right. It's December 15th. I leave tonight for the Dominican Republic. I'm not there yet.*

He took a few more long drags on the cigarette, butted it in the ashtray and returned to bed.

He drifted into a restless sleep and images of people chasing him haunted his subconscious.

He awoke at 6:45 am. thinking that something just wasn't right.

But he couldn't put a finger on it.

He made some coffee, sat at his desk reviewing his itinerary. Nels lived in Woodlands, a middle class suburban neighborhood. He had renovated his large bungalow to his tastes, painting it in deep green tones, after purchasing it four years ago. He loved the vibe of the house, in spite of all his nightmares. He didn't blame the house for that. It was part of his fucked up psyche.

Although he was doing mainly freelance writing for websites currently, he hoped one day his home would be the place where he would create a great novel.

He had always fancied himself a writer but could never bring himself to concentrate long enough to get anything other than a basic story line on paper.

Besides, his life was a little boring in Calgary anyway. He didn't find a lot of inspiration in his day-to-day grind.

He hoped this year would be different. Or, if not, next year was just around the corner.

He checked his itinerary and groaned. He would leave tonight at 7:10 p.m. and take a flight from Calgary International Airport to the Ottawa's MacDonald-Cartier International Airport. The flight would arrive at one in the morning, three hours ahead of Calgary time. His next flight would be Continental Flight 4298 to Newark Liberty International Airport at 6:15 a.m., which meant he had to spend at least five hours hanging around Ottawa airport.

It wasn't enough time to get a hotel and it was barely enough time to sleep.

Luckily, his connecting flight from Newark called for a short seventy five minute layover, before arriving at Puerto Plata's Gregorio Luperon Airport at 2:23p.m., just under twenty four hours from when he would leave.

He scratched his two-day growth and worked on his last article. An hour later, he walked into the kitchen. He poured a Muslix cereal mix into a bowl, chopped up a banana, added some milk and carried the concoction into his office. He continued with the last minute details of his trip while he ate.

Well-travelled, Nels had been to the DR before and he liked the country. He knew the dangers but had street smarts and a good grasp of Spanish, which had served him well in the past.

Although he didn't do the five-star all-inclusive thing, which gave a person a completely different perspective of the island, he loved the beautiful beaches, the friendliness of the locals, the culture and the weather. At 43, he considered himself too young to settle down in Canada and he craved adventure-which he found a lot of in the DR.

On previous trips, he had volunteered to help build houses for the poor-and there were many.

He suddenly remembered he had two calls to make. And he wasn't looking forward to either one.

He dialed his Dominican girlfriend Novelee first. As he listened to the phone ring he wondered how the conversation would play out. Lately, the conversations had revolved around her problems with money and her health. She had a thyroid problem and the pills she was taking weren't working.

Nels had sent a number of payments, including $1,700 for major dental work, but he wondered if or when it would end.

She picked up the phone. "Hola," she said. She did not speak English.

"How are you doing sweetie?" Nels asked in Spanish.

"I'm here in my house," Novelee said.

Lately, she never seemed to be doing well when he asked. It was always, 'I'm here.' Which meant she wasn't doing well. She had no work, her thyroid condition created many sleepless nights, and she couldn't find work.

She said something else and Nels couldn't make it out. A bad connection, or a cheap cell phone on her end. Nels had just bought new cordless phones and the phone company had tested things after he accidentally disconnected one of the lines during a renovation. So he knew the problem wasn't on his end.

"What's that honey? I can't hear you."

Her voice rose a few decibels and became agitated. "I'm here, at home, in my bed. You don't understand me?"

Nels became impatient, a little out of sorts from his nightmare. His voice became agitated. "I can understand you quite well when I can hear you, but how do you expect me to understand you if I can't hear you?"

"You don't have to raise your voice."

Nels instantly felt bad. After all, she had become quite ill with her thyroid condition and he had heard that sometimes such a condition could mess with a woman's emotions and moods. He remembered a friend telling him once, that his wife would swing from happy to sad to agitated all in the course of an hour due to her thyroid problem.

"I'm sorry honey," Nels said. "Let's back this up. I'm calling to tell you I will finally be coming to the DR."

"When?" she asked.

"I arrive in Puerto Plata tomorrow afternoon at about three."

"That's great. I'm looking forward to seeing you. Where will you be staying?"

"In Costambar, but I still haven't been able to find an apartment. Are you going to be meeting me at the airport?" Nels asked.

"How am I going to do that with no money?"

Nels thought he had better leave that one alone. It had been awhile since he had sent her any money via Western Union. Without cab fare, she would have to wait until he arrived to pay the driver. And if the plane was late, the meter would probably continue to run. You never know in the DR. Besides, Nels had an ex-military cab driver, Jose, who had showed him his hand cannon on previous trips and said if he had to, he would defend him with his life. Jose had proven to be a loyal ally and over the years Nels had sent him plenty of business. God knew-you needed a few loyal allies in the DR, particularly on the crazy north shore.

Nels knew he could arrange for Jose to first pick up Novelee and then arrive at the airport but the whole plan was starting to become way too complicated. It would be much easier to arrive in Puerto Plata, have Jose pick him up, secure an apartment in Costambar and then call his girlfriend. She could then hop on a cheap "motoconcho" taxi, arrive at the apartment and Nels could flip the driver a hundred peso note, about two dollars and sixty cents Canadian, and that would be the end of it.

"No problem honey. Once I get a room I'll call you and you can come over," Nels said.

"Yes, no problem." There was a long pause and then Novelee finally said. "Listen there are many things I have to tell you when you arrive."

"Like what?" Nels asked.

"I have a lot of crazy bad things in my mind lately. I'm not working, I can't find a job, I'm losing weight because of my thyroid. And I'm thinking all the time. Thinking of crazy, bad things."

Nels still had a lot of things to do before boarding his planes later that day. And his nightmare had made him almost afraid to ask. "Well get those crazy things out of your mind and start thinking positive. If you think negative all the time it becomes a self-fulfilling prophecy and you'll attract bad energy. Bad things will start to happen to you."

"You're right I should let them go. But it's not easy. I have so many problems in my life right now. I will tell you about all the bad stuff later."

Nels wasn't sure he wanted to hear it. But, in their three years together, which amounted to the two or three months a year Nels spent in the DR, he was convinced he had a loyal woman. Albeit, hot tempered and extremely feisty.

"Listen babe, I have to go now, I have to make some calls and pack my stuff." They exchanged a few terms of endearment, some x-rated, and Nels hung up the phone.

He breathed a deep sigh of relief and paused before making his second call. Something about the nightmare seemed eerily real and he wondered if he should just cancel his plans, suffer a frigid winter in Calgary and get to work on his novel on safe, luxurious and comfortable home soil.

"Ahh to hell with it," he said aloud and picked up the phone.

Belinda answered. "Nels, how are you?"

He decided to leave out details about the nightmare, at least for now. "I'm great. Are we still on for dinner?"

"For sure," Belinda said. "We're both looking forward to seeing you." They had made an arrangement to keep an eye on Nels' home and drive him to the airport. "Is six okay for us to pick you up?"

"It's going to have to be a lot earlier than that," Nels said, detecting a slightly irritated tone in Belinda's voice that he hadn't noticed in the past. He thought there might be a problem in their relationship, but dared not to ask. "My flight leaves at seven."

"Okay, I'll pick you up at two thirty, we can have a quick bite to eat at my place, then we'll get you off to the airport."

"See you then sweetie," Nels said and hung up the phone.

A few hours later he sat at Simon and Belinda's dinner table in their 2,500 square foot tastefully decorated bungalow in Woodlands Estates.

Belinda heaped a large spoon of spaghetti onto his plate and passed over the salad. Simon eyed the portion and frowned. "Can you eat all that?" he asked Nels.

"I'll try," Nels said, switching his gaze from Simon and back to Belinda.

"Honey, you should let the guests serve themselves," Simon said. "He can't eat all that."

Belinda ignored the comment and smiled at Nels, showing the small gap between her two front teeth that Nels found so attractive. In her mid-forties, Belinda was very cute, if not beautiful. Her white freckled complexion, penetrating blue eyes and wavy blonde hair probably turned many heads. It didn't hurt that her five foot four frame was well proportioned and only beginning to show a few signs of age, a very slight belly that Nels knew Belinda was self-conscious about, but he felt suited her perfectly and accentuated her other attractive body parts.

Simon began digging into his meal. About six foot three and 190 pounds, he was an athletic and outspoken man who owned his own debt collection business. Although fifty, he could easily pass for thirty-five. His calm demeanor belied his potential for aggression and Nels knew he ran a tight ship and was one of the best in the city at collecting unpaid debts.

He had an olive toned complexion, brown eyes, short cropped black hair and an easy smile. At least, most of the time. Today he looked slightly agitated and Nels felt uneasy.

Belinda owned a temporary placement center that she had started about six years ago. By all accounts, it was doing quite well. Between the two of them, they brought in a respectable income. And, with no kids and a sharp eye for budgeting, they would probably be looking to retire within the next three years.

"I don't want to talk a lot of shop," Belinda said, between bites of her salad. "But I just hired five more temps today and it brings the total to forty."

Nels had his mouth full so he just smiled. As he chewed he thought about the number forty. He remembered an Asian friend telling him one time that the Chinese viewed the number four with particular dislike. Apparently, it was one of the worst numbers in Chinese numerology and particularly bad were number combinations that contained more than one number four. To the Chinese it meant death, disease, and financial ruin, along with a host of other calamities.

Nels didn't want to read too much into it, as he knew a superstition about certain number combinations could become a self-fulfilling prophecy. But the education he had received from his friend left him thinking about the numbers when he did encounter them. And, a few times the number combinations figured in his nightmares.

He also remembered chatting to a woman he had met in a coffee shop a few weeks back and she had laid out a sad story about her husband's worsening health, a house that seemed to be falling apart, and major discord developing in the relationship. She looked frail and sad and had asked Nels if he could refer her to a good realtor as her worsening financial situation had made it mandatory that she sell her house.

Out of curiosity Nels asked the address. He couldn't remember the street now but he definitely remembered the house number.

404.

Although he had a few close friends who were realtors, he didn't want them involved in any way with the property. So, he quietly told her he didn't have any connections.

"You're off in a fog," Belinda said, watching his green eyes stare around the room. "Did you even hear what I just said?"

Nels blinked. "Yeah I did; Five new temps. That's awesome. Congratulations." He lifted his glass of white wine, toasted the two. "Cheers to your success."

Belinda's tone suddenly changed. "I wanted to talk to you about your Dominican girlfriend."

Nels had mentioned when he had first arrived at Belinda's that the last conversation had left him uneasy about his travel plans. He stared at Belinda.

She continued. "She's not your equal Nels. You're a good-looking guy and an intellectual at that. How long do you think you can last with a poverty stricken, uneducated woman like her? I know you can speak Spanish and all, but how far do you see it going? I mean you certainly can't have any deep conversations with her."

The conversation piqued Simon's interest and he looked up from his meal at Nels.

"What do you suggest I do?" Nels asked.

"Well, enjoy your time with her, that's all. I'm sure she's got a hot little body, so have some good sex, have some fun with her and forget about her when you get back. But don't try reading any more into it than that."

Nels had been considering a more permanent relationship with Novelee for the last couple of years. He had plans to liquidate some of his real estate holdings and move to the DR, if not on a permanent basis, at least for six months of the year. As a writer, he could pretty much work anywhere in the world.

"Maybe you're right," he said, scratching his two-day growth and adjusting his glasses.

"I am right," Belinda said. "It's woman's intuition."

"Well for whatever reason, I can't seem to find a Canadian girlfriend. Maybe it's my fucked up psyche or the fact that I like being by myself so often, but it isn't happening for me."

"When you're ready to have a relationship with a woman here, you'll find one. You're not ready, that's all," Belinda said. "You like adventure and travel too much."

"Well I have this thing about loyalty," Nels said. "I've been seeing Novelee for three years and I haven't cheated on her."

"Well cheat on her. Have some fun for a change. Those long distance things never work anyway. And what she doesn't know won't hurt her."

They finished dinner and Nels helped them clean the dishes and load the leftovers into plastic containers. He had only eaten half of his large portion and Simon grimaced slightly but told him to throw it in the garbage can.

"I hate wasting food," Simon said.

They moved into the comfortable living room arranged with three large black leather sofas and chatted about Nels' trip, details about Belinda's role in looking after his house, and then they began a conversation about the nature of relationships, friendship and otherwise.

"I think maybe I'm just not cut out for a relationship," Nels said. "Every time one seems to get too serious, I seem to find a way to push the woman away and end it. Typical male commitment issues."

"When you're ready, it'll happen," Belinda said.

Simon looked bored throughout the conversation and stood up. "I'm going into the office to make a few calls."

"Now?" Belinda asked, raising an eyebrow. "Why don't you stay here and keep us company?"

"No, I have some calls to make."

"To whom?"

"I'm going to call some family I haven't talked to for awhile. My brother for one."

Belinda frowned as Simon left. "You think he could sit here and entertain us?"

"It's okay with me," Nels said. "If he has his own thing to do, I'm happy enough with your company anyway."

"Happy enough? What, you don't find me interesting?"

"Of course I do. I didn't mean it that way."

Chapter Four

11:56 pm, Thursday, December 15th, 2011, Sosua, Dominican Republic. A seedy hooker bar on Calle Pedro Clisante.

Through an alcoholic haze, Heinz Schmitt eyed the young woman stationed at the corner of the bar. She looked no older than nineteen, he thought, maybe a little younger.

It was his fifth day in Sosua, a town on the north coast with a population of about 50,000, depending on who you talked to. The town's nickname-Sosewer, had been coined by someone from the large ex-pat community, a long time ago. No one seemed to know who coined it, but it had stuck. It was a gutter for prostitution, thieves, murderers and crazy ex-pats who knew only too well they could move here, behave like drunken, asshole zombies and probably get away with it. That is, unless they went too far. Then they would wind up dead.

On the upside, Sosua also housed a responsible and supportive ex-pat community and a number of trustworthy locals. It also had nice beaches, some good restaurants and bars and could be a lot of fun.

Fabiola winked at Heinz and he smiled. She smiled back, exposing a mouthful of braces. Salsa music thumped from the large speakers and motoconchos raced up and down the street. The noise pollution was deafening and half the time the only way the sex tourists could handle it is if they were half, or entirely in the bag.

Heinz was only half in the bag, or so he reasoned, when he staggered up to the bar and offered to buy her a drink. His Spanish wasn't half bad and he seemed to think the drunker he got, the better his Spanish became. Since his arrival from Germany, he had already slept with fourteen hookers. He was averaging three a day, one in the early morning, one in the late afternoon and another in the late evening.

Other than a late night problem with one hooker freaking out and demanding more money in the middle of the night, Heinz's sexual escapades had been problem free. And all it had taken to get rid of and shut up that psycho hooker was one thousand pesos. Problem solved.

He had already notched his two for today and went to work on the third. Two Bohemias showed up, were plunked on the table, Heinz paid for them and the sexy and scantily clad bartender disappeared with a smile. And a wink.

He eyed up the hooker. She had flowing long black hair, dark skin and was obviously Dominican and not Haitian. Their skin tone was typically a lot darker in color.

She had cute brown eyes, an innocent smile, large breasts and a proportionate body type. Heinz had a thing for big tits.

He clinked beers with Fabiola and made introductions. She looked at him curiously as she talked and he wondered if she even knew what he was saying or could even hear him.

He decided to go to the bathroom and cut to the chase on his return. In the bathroom he smiled at himself in the mirror as he urinated. Deeply etched lines in his face spoke of years of partying and late nights. His gray beard and scraggly gray hair made him look much older than his fifty years. He could easily pass for sixty-five.

"I'm going to fuck this one all night long," he said to himself through bloodshot eyes.

A small Dominican man walked into the bathroom and gave him a strange look, as if taking offense to the word fuck. Heinz knew that was one word they all seemed to understand, so he cut his oratory short, finished urinating, zipped up his fly, and walked back to the table.

He smiled as he sat next to Fabiola and she returned the favor.

As the music thumped, his mind drifted. *Shit*, he thought. *I was supposed to call my wife and kids in Germany this afternoon and I forgot.* Heinz worked as a musician and the story he had given his wife and two daughters was that he needed some inspiration to write a few songs, so he had booked a holiday in the Sewer.

Maybe I'll just fuck her for a few hours and then call the family, he decided, unable to put together the time difference. The Dominican fog was enveloping him.

"Stay on guard," he said to no one in particular. "You're in the DR."

Fabiola's brow wrinkled. "I didn't understand you," she said in Spanish.

He leaned over, put his arm around her and kissed her full on the mouth. She responded in kind, slipping him the tongue. Her hand slid across his knee and expertly glided its way to his crotch.

He felt the stirrings of sexual desire. "How much for the night?"

"Two thousand pesos."

That was common. They would always start high.

"One thousand," he said, cupping one of her breasts.

She smiled again and pushed his hand to the other breast, allowing him a full sample of her firmness. "Fifteen hundred," she said, not wanting to waste any more time.

"Good enough," Heinz said. He stood up and took her by the hand. They walked out of the bar with their beers, Heinz staggering, and Fabiola supporting him.

Eduardo watched as they left. When they were half a block away, he paid his bill and followed, keeping a safe distance behind them.

Twenty minutes later, Heinz was sprawled out on his back, naked. Fabiola, on top, humped away while he fondled her massive breasts. The bed creaked. Heinz grunted with pleasure.

Fabiola made not a sound. With her deadpan expression, she could have been watching a soap opera.

Heinz finished with a large grunt. Fabiola watched him for a few minutes until his eyes closed. It didn't take long. He was an easy mark.

She went to the door and opened it. Eduardo, his slender five foot four frame contradicting the savagery he was capable of, ran into the room while Fabiola quickly locked the door.

She thought about getting dressed but then decided she would rather enjoy the action in the nude-at least for a little while. She turned on the TV, turned the volume up.

Eduardo walked to the bedside, producing a small wooden baseball bat. Just as Heinz noticed some commotion and began opening his eyes, he smashed him in the head with it-just hard enough to show him who was in charge.

In a few minutes Heinz was bound and gagged spread eagle on the bed. Eduardo threw a small towel over his privates. He had no interest in men. The two flipped the room upside down, discovered about 10,000 pesos and about $271.00 US, hidden in a flip up plastic cover inside the TV. Behind the plastic cover were control knobs for dimming and brightness.

Fabiola had positioned a chair at the foot of the bed now and watched as Eduardo continued to interrogate Heinz. He wanted a bank card and a pin number or he wouldn't be happy.

Problem was, Heinz had left his passport, along with credit cards, bank cards and more cash at the hotel reception for safekeeping. It wasn't in the room.

Eduardo handed Fabiola a large knife and motioned to her. She walked over to the bedside and held it to Heinz's throat, telling him his mouth gag would be removed and if he screamed he would be dead.

He stared at her with bulging eyes and nodded. She removed the gag. He coughed and spittle dripped down his face and onto his neck.

Eduardo wacked him in the head with the small bat, causing a small cut that spurted blood. Heinz grunted.

"Tell me where your bank card and other money is," Eduardo demanded, standing over him with the bat while Fabiola pushed the knife slightly into his jugular, just hard enough to make him wince.

"It's not here. It's downstairs at the reception. You let me go. I'll get it all for you. Just don't kill me," Heinz pleaded.

Eduardo clenched the bat, his fingers whitening with the force. He smashed Heinz in the nose with it and blood squirted out. His broken nose slanted to the left. "I don't believe you. Where is the rest of your money?"

Heinz had to clear his throat and spit the blood before speaking. "I told you. It's downstairs at reception."

Eduardo wasn't buying it. He smashed Heinz in the face with the bat again, knocking two teeth into his mouth and two more flying across the small room.

Heinz spit out two teeth, along with a mouthful of blood. His skin had turned an ashen white. He panicked and started screaming. He only got about one tenth of a second into the shriek before Fabiola smiled and sliced open his jugular vein.

Chapter Five

3:34 pm, Friday, December 16, Gregorio Luperon Airport, Puerto Plata, DR.

The plane touched down on the tarmac with a loud bang. It had smoothly descended through the popcorn clouds and blue sky, but the landing hadn't been so smooth. It was a balmy 27 degrees Celsius and there was a gentle breeze blowing.

By the time he would reach Costambar, Nels would have been travelling for more than twenty- four hours. The first leg of the flight from Calgary to Ottawa was a nightmare. A woman with two kids, boy and girl aged about eight and nine, had sat across the aisle from him. She had positioned her young boy beside Nels and he squirmed in his seat the whole trip and complained. She had tried switching her daughter to the seat and that resulted in an angry outburst of crying.

Why the fuck doesn't she sit beside me, put the two kids together across the aisle from her, and let me get some sleep?

The five-hour layover in Ottawa had gone slightly better. Nels had found a rather secluded couch and had been able to curl up for a few hours before waking up in a cold sweat, a fresh image of a baseball bat connecting with someone's unfortunate head.

The nightmare had stayed with him and left him unsettled. So he had gotten up, walked around and finally found a Tim Horton's coffee shop that was open twenty-four hours. He sat down and quickly made friends with a native Indian miner and a secretary from Calgary. He had spent the better part of two hours chatting with them before boarding his connection to Newark.

The three had become such fast friends they had even exchanged contact information, vowing to keep in touch. *That was the great thing about travelling,* Nels thought. *You never knew how the people you met would change the course of your life.*

But he couldn't seem to get the unsettling image of the baseball bat out of his mind.

A man bumped him in the head with his suitcase, ending the daydream. "I'm sorry," he said. Nels stood up, reaching for his laptop carrying case and small knapsack.

Fifteen minutes later, he walked out into the fresh air of the DR, feeling mentally and physically exhausted. *I need to get some sleep,* he thought as Jose approached him with a smile and a handshake. *I hope I can sleep.*

He hopped in the white minivan without clearly marked taxi signs and Jose pulled out.

Nels was a part-time insomniac and occasionally on his trips to the DR he would need Zopiclone to knock himself out. Sometimes the schizophrenic nature of the country caused his mind to race and he couldn't turn it off. Occasionally, he would need sleeping pills and plenty of rum to pass out.

As Jose drove, Nels wondered if this trip would be the same. He remembered on the last trip after he and Novelee had adjusted to each other's sleeping patterns and presence, he had done quite well. In fact, he had only needed the sleeping pills about five times.

Not bad for a part-time insomniac.

Still unaccustomed to living with anyone, he found the best course of action was to have Novelee stay with him for two nights and then he would send her home for two nights to deal with her family and nine year old son Papito

"How was your trip?" Jose asked, as Nels stared out the window zombie-like.

He smiled. "Good. I'm exhausted though. Travelling for twenty four hours with no sleep."

Jose sighed and gave him a sympathetic look. They exchanged some small talk in Spanish, and then Nels gave Jose the travel instructions. Three stops-one to activate a Dominican phone, the other to pick up some staples, beer and rum and last stop Atlantic One, Costambar, where Nels had managed to secure six nights before he would have to hunt for other accommodations.

As the snowbirds flocked to the beachfront gated beach community of Costambar, decent apartments were getting harder and harder to find. The relative tranquility of the small town on the fringe of Puerto Plata, with a population of around 2,000, attracted many foreigners. They loved the beaches, the diverse culture, the weather and the strong ex-pat community. It didn't hurt that it was very cheap to live there.

Forty minutes later, Jose pulled up to the Atlantic One and Nels got out. He set his bag containing rum, fruit juices and toilet paper down and Jose carried out the small knapsack and laptop case. Nels had packed a cheap travel laptop he had purchased on Kijiji before arriving and he had also brought a netbook-just in case he had a problem with the cheapie.

Jose's normal rate for a Puerto Plata airport pick-up and delivery to Costambar was five hundred pesos. But, with all the stops, a large tip was in order.

Nels had always admired Jose for his work ethic. He owned one rental property in Puerto Plata, another in the small town of Montellano, where he lived with his wife and two kids. He also owned a cellular shop, his cab business and was in his second year studying to be a corporate lawyer.

Even if his trips with Nels required him to stop and wait awhile, he never drank alcohol on the job. Orange juice and water was all Nels had ever seen him drink, although he had yet to take him up on an invitation to have dinner with his family.

Jose liked Chivas Regal and beer. He wasn't a rum drinker, insisting Brugal caused major hangovers and headaches.

Jose carried the bags into the main floor one bedroom apartment and Nels followed with the booze. He walked back outside the gated set of buildings and fished in his pocket for some money.

"How much?" he asked. But lately Jose would never tell him how much. He considered himself a good friend of Nels.

"You just give me what you think is fair and what you can afford and I'll be happy," Jose said. "With normal customers, I'll quote a price, but you're a friend."

With an unknown cab driver this strategy would never wash. But Jose and Nels had history.

He peeled off two five hundred notes. "Is this okay? Because I want you to tell me if you think it's not enough."

"It's fine," Jose said, his expression not giving away anything.

It was the first time he had stayed at Atlantic One and he liked it already. He sat on his main floor balcony and surveyed the surroundings, listening to the crickets while waiting for Novelee to arrive. The pool was large, had a number of bed-style lawn chairs strategically arranged and the management had recently installed actual beds with umbrellas for the guests.

A few twinkling red lights wrapped around palm trees gave the complex a romantic, safe and sexy feel.

Considered one of the better managed and quieter locations in Costambar, Atlantic One consisted of three buildings, each containing six small apartments. It was equipped with a reasonably priced restaurant and bar. High season day rates ranged from $45 to $65 US per night while long-term monthly rates were around $500 to $650 US per month. This included electricity, internet and cable TV.

An hour and a half later, Nels smiled as he noticed an eight ball attached to the key ring of his room.

"Number eight," he said aloud, pouring his second rum and fruit punch. "That's a good number."

Although he had some doubts about Novelee on the phone recently, they began to evaporate as he imagined her slender body acrobatically performing for him under the sheets.

He felt the stirring of desire and smiled, anxiously awaiting her arrival.

Chapter Six

10:26 pm, Friday, December 16th, Sol y Mio Italian Restaurant, Costambar.

Nels looked at Novelee through foggy lenses as she ate her meal. It was the alcohol and lack of sleep that made the lenses foggy. He took a bite of his pizza and watched her eat her pork chops, potatoes and vegetables. She ate quickly, shoveling the food into her mouth. He wondered when she had last eaten. She did not look up to talk, and Nels knew better than to interrupt her while she ate.

He had tried conversation during a meal last year and she had politely told him that in her culture when people ate they didn't talk.

After he processed the information, he realized that at her level of poverty, when she got a meal on her plate, she would have to wolf it down, not knowing when the next one would be coming or if someone was going to steal it out from under her if she didn't eat it quick enough.

He knew she sometimes went days without food, sometimes subsisting on just rice.

So much for a romantic dinner, he thought, looking around at the candlelit tables. There were about six other couples in the restaurant and they joked and laughed while they ate and drank.

Soft music, unidentifiable to Nels, played.

When she finally finished, he asked, "So, you mentioned some problems on the phone but we didn't get into it. What happened?"

He tried to keep his eyes from her ample cleavage while she talked. Novelee was 32 and she could pass for about 25. She had long black hair and a slender but shapely body. Her breasts, while relatively small, were perfectly shaped. She had beautiful brown eyes and thanks to a recent expenditure on Nels' part, a perfect set of white teeth. Her face beamed when she smiled.

But she wasn't smiling as she recounted her life over the last couple of months.

There had been a disagreement with her sister, two years her junior. Apparently, Gloria had accused Novelee of stealing her cell phone and Novelee had beaten the shit out of her-on two separate occasions. For her trouble, she had spent two days in jail.

She finished the story by telling Nels that her sister had even slept with one of her previous boyfriends.

Nels had met Gloria. He thought she was a hard working Christian, much different than other predatory female Dominican women he had met. Gloria cleaned homes and worked hard to support her two small children, on an island that had one of the highest poverty rates in the entire Caribbean.

Even through his foggy lenses, Nels could tell that Novelee was getting drunk. All of ninety five pounds, she was a lightweight when it came to alcohol consumption.

"Are you asking for my opinion of your behavior?" he finally asked, taking a long pull on his Cuba libre.

"No," she said matter-of-factly. "I'm telling you how I am. So you know now. Maybe you don't want a woman like me with all my problems."

Nels didn't know what to say. And, right now, he didn't want to piss her off.

"I don't have any patience for people who screw me over," she said. "And anyone who does is going to have hell to pay for it. I'll get even with them, one way or another. And I'm even thinking of tracking down the father of my kid, get him to pay some money, or I'll kill him."

Nels knew Novelee had been married to a Dominican man who had abused her and quickly abandoned her after the birth of Papito

"That wouldn't be too smart," he said.

"Well, he abandoned us and he needs to pay."

"I'm sure if you found him, he wouldn't have any money anyway," Nels said, beginning for the first time to fear for his safety with this woman whom he thought he knew so well.

But, he wanted to push the issue to see if she showed even an inkling of remorse. "Do you think that's okay what you did to your sister? Is that what you think? There are a lot of people I don't like, who have ripped me off and done other things but I can't go around kicking the shit out of them. If I did I'd end up dead, beat up badly, or in jail."

"Well that's just the way I am," she said. "If you think I have too many problems you are free to find yourself another girlfriend."

In his drunken and fatigued state, Nels thought perhaps it was better to let dead dogs lie.

He paid the bill, left the restaurant and they walked back to the apartment. In spite of the news, he couldn't wait to get her undressed and into his bedroom, not necessarily in that order.

I must be crazy, he thought.

They made love. It wasn't quite like Nels had remembered. Okay, but far from great. When they finished, Novelee got up, walked into the living room and curled up on the couch. She knew from previous experiences with Nels he liked his privacy and often had trouble sleeping if someone was in the same bed with him.

Besides, when he had his nightmares he often talked in his sleep and flailed his arms. She had been the recipient of a few well-placed but unintended blows.

Chapter Seven

2:33 am, Saturday, December 17th, New York City, USA.

Nels couldn't be sure if he was dreaming or not. He was lost in a big modern city, New York or somewhere, he had no idea.

He walked the streets trying to figure out where he was and how to get home. *Again, where was home exactly?*

He walked down the street searching for a bus or a taxi that could take him who knew where. He tried to flag a taxi but none of them would stop. He saw a number 44 on a bus and ran to catch it. The bus stopped abruptly and the kindly driver opened the door and smiled at him.

He was a short man, about five-foot fuck-all, with a toothy grin and jet black hair, comb-over style. "Where you off to my friend?" the bus driver asked.

"Umm, I'm trying to catch a plane I think."

"You think. Well if you don't know than how the hell should I know?" Suddenly the man's face contorted into a clown and he started laughing at Nels. Soon, all the people on the bus were laughing.

What am I thinking? That's number 44.

He turned and ran across the street, a few cars narrowly missing him and honking.

You're dreaming. Wake up. But he couldn't. Fuck, not again.

Maybe I didn't get off the flight? That's it, I'm in Newark, but somehow I left the airport. I just have to get back, get my connection to Puerto Plata.

He stopped beside a young attractive woman in black business attire. "How do I get to the airport in Newark?"

"It's that way," she said, pointing up in the sky.

Nels searched the sky for answers and found none.

Then her face transformed into an ugly gray witch and she smiled, a mocking smile showing oversized rotten teeth.

She cackled at Nels and handed him a broom. "It's up there, here take this." And she cackled some more.

He turned and ran down the street. He approached a busy intersection, thought the pedestrian sign displayed green, then at the last minute, noticed it was red.

Red meant stop.

But it was too late. In the middle of the intersection, he looked right at the last second and saw a bus, barreling toward him, the number 44 glowing ominously and the clown-faced driver laughing as it rapidly approached.

A split second before the bus could smash into him, Nels jerked upright in his bed, soaked in sweat, his heart pounding. He was about to scream when he realized where he was.

There was a dull throbbing in his head, the result of too much Brugal rum. He had heard a few of the locals refer to it as Brutal and now he understood why. Maybe Jose was right. He walked into the kitchen and checked his watch.

3:46 am.

He walked into the bathroom, relieved himself, went into the kitchen and opened the fridge. He realized he had forgotten to buy water and pulled out a container of Rica pear juice. He noticed Novelee sleeping peacefully on the couch as he drank from the container. Or at least she looked to be sleeping peacefully.

He walked into the bathroom again, remembering he had brought two sleeping pills with him for emergency. He made a mental note to buy some more at the pharmacy later. He pulled one out of its cellophane wrapping and placed it on his tongue, enjoying the acidy taste for a moment before swallowing it with the pear juice.

He returned to bed wondering what the significance of the nightmare might be. He always tried to find meaning in them.

Only one word came to mind.

Two-faced.

Chapter Eight

10:45 am, Saturday, December 17th, Atlantic One, apartment number eight, Costambar.

Nels woke up groggy from the pills, a few too many drinks and too many travel hours the night before without sleep. He was still playing catch up. He hated taking the sleeping pills, as typically the after effects would leave him feeling groggy and tired for most of the day.

He doubted today would be any exception as he walked into the shower and turned the cold water on. *Maybe a cold shower would clear the cobwebs?*

He finished showering, went into the living room and sat down. Novelee already had the television turned on and was watching some Spanish novella.

"How are you sweetie?" he asked.

"I hardly got any sleep. And you?"

"A fitful sleep. Feels like I need more."

"I have been thinking of another job opportunity," she said.

"Oh, what's that?"

"There are two discos in Cabarete looking for waitresses."

Nels knew that typically waitresses in discos also served as prostitutes, with the establishment acting as pimps and collecting an exit fee. "I don't know if that's the best idea."

"Well do you have any other ideas? I have a nice body, very nice breasts and many men tell me I'm attractive."

"What about disease?"

"That is one thing that worries me. I don't want to get sick. But I think I'll go to the interview anyway."

Nels didn't really have the mindset to start voicing any major opposition. His head was still swimming a bit. "Suit yourself. But I do not like the idea." He knew if she acquired any such work he would drop her like a lead balloon.

Her mind had begun to work in strange and mysterious ways. But he also knew she had lost a lot of weight and the thyroid condition could be completely messing with her head.

He gave here the benefit of the doubt. For now.

She showered and they went out for breakfast at a small restaurant close to Yenny's Supermarket. After awhile, Novelee asked Nels if his friend would be arriving soon.

"Yes, he is, he just doesn't have a flight date yet."

"Do you still want me to hook him up with one of my friends?"

This had been a topic of conversation for some months before the trip and Nels had commissioned Novelee to find a girlfriend for his friend Wilson.

Nels hesitated for a moment. "Okay sure, just make sure it's someone good."

"I have one in mind but I don't know that she'll work, so I might find another one."

"I'll leave that up to you."

They finished breakfast and Novelee said she had to go home to do laundry.

Nels was happy to hear this, as he wanted to make a few phone calls and have some time to himself. He flipped her a thousand pesos, kissed her, and waited for her reaction.

She stared at him blankly.

"Do you not say thank you in the Dominican Republic?" he asked. It annoyed him when he had to remind her to thank him for money. She never thanked him for all the meals he bought her and he didn't even bother reminding her on those occasions.

"Thank you," she said.

He watched her walk toward the gates, where she would take a carro-publico into Puerto Plata for 25 pesos.

As he turned to walk back to his apartment, he noticed a small Dominican man eyeing him, with more than a casual interest. Dominicans often stared at gringos. We're just different. But, the cold stare he was getting gave him a creepy feeling.

He couldn't be sure, but he thought he knew him from somewhere. He ended the eye contact quickly, turned and walked back to Atlantic One.

Eduardo pulled his phone from his pocket and punched in some numbers. "I can see him. I know what he looks like now. Novelee is on her way home." He clicked the phone shut and smiled.

Sitting in her dumpy one room apartment in Puerto Plata, Fabiola smiled as she hung up.

Chapter Nine

3:56 pm, Saturday, December 17th, Catamaran Restaurant, beachfront, Costambar.

Nels sat with a few of his ex-pat friends and sipped on a Bohemia. He had just eaten the *plato del dia,* which consisted of chicken, rice, beans and a side salad for 150 pesos. A great price and awesome food. He was getting caught up on the local gossip from Bill and Linda, snowbirds from Toronto who had just retired and now spent six to seven months of the year in Costambar.

Nels had returned home to Atlantic One, checked his emails and made some Skype calls. His friend Wilson had finally booked his arrival date-December 29th. That meant Nels would be busy arranging airport pick up and trying to get Wilson a reasonably priced apartment.

Another friend from Sweden, Jonas, would also be arriving on the 29th and planned on staying in Sosua. Jonas was an accountant and was adept at navigating the dangerous waters of Sosewer.

Considering himself too young to settle down, Jonas loved the adventure of sleeping with hookers and enjoyed the thrill having multiple partners. He also volunteered his services in the community, often helping to build houses for the poor or volunteering in a local medical clinic.

They often joked that Jonas was the gold medal champion of the Sosewer Olympics and his return trip would be an attempt to hang onto his gold medal by sleeping with as many women as possible in a short amount of time.

They had agreed to hook up on New Year's Eve in Costambar.

The last call he made was the one that had rattled him. Belinda had said they were planning to join him in Costambar. They had booked a flight for January 3rd, and would be staying at the Seahorse condos in Costambar.

Nels couldn't help thinking he should have told them about his nightmare while he was still in Calgary. Maybe it would have prompted them to change their plans? When he had mentioned it on the phone, Belinda had dismissed it and laughed, saying she would not be frightened easily.

They were coming and there wasn't a thing he could do about it.

Nels heard someone say "dead" and took his eyes away from the waves. He loved looking at the Atlantic Ocean, listening to the crashing sound of waves. He had always found it mesmerizing.

"What did you say?" he asked Bill.

"We saw a dead man on the beach this morning. Washed up on shore, lying on his belly. Everyone just sat there for about an hour and finally someone realized he wasn't moving, so they called the police."

"Do you know any details?" Nels asked, taking a long sip of his beer and motioning for the waitress to bring another one.

"Well from what I heard he drowned while swimming. Apparently he was a strong swimmer but who knows? I also heard he was a friend of one of the Russians living here."

"Go figure," Nels said. "The very next day after I arrive someone turns up dead on the beach."

"That's not all," Linda said, holding up the peace sign to the waitress indicating she wanted two more beers.

The waitress put three cold beers on the table and left.

"What else?" Nels asked, picking up his beer and tilting it back.

"A tourist got killed in Sosua couple days ago. Bound, gagged, beaten and his throat was slit," Linda said.

"Well shit at least the weather's nice," Nels said, attempting to lighten the mood. But he was having a hard time doing it.

"What are you doing for Christmas?" Linda asked, smiling. Her smile was infectious.

"No plans yet," Nels said. "Playing it by ear. And you?"

"Oh we have some family coming in, so we'll be entertaining at our condo."

Ten minutes later Nels had paid for his beer and walked along the beach, enjoying the feeling of the sand and warm ocean water on his feet. He thought he saw some friends at another beach side bar and walked over to see if it was them.

Once he got closer, he realized it was not his ex-pat friends, but another group whom he did not know. He contemplated ordering another beer, when a grey-haired man, probably in his 50's, motioned to him. The slightly overweight man sat by himself at a table drinking a Presidente Grande and smiling at Nels.

"How's it going? You look lost."

"No, I just thought I spotted some friends here, but then I realized it wasn't them."

"Nothing like having a beer in paradise," the man said.

"You got that right," Nels said.

"Want to join me?"

"I might go back for a nap. Just got in yesterday and I'm still playing catch-up."

"I'm Mitch," the man said, extending his hand.

Nels shook it. "Nels. Where you from?"

"I live in Billings, Montana. And you?"

"I'm from Calgary."

"Oh, I was born in Calgary," Mitch said.

Something about this guy just didn't feel right to Nels. "You spend a lot of time down here?"

"I come down six to seven months of the year," Mitch said.

"Did you find a decent apartment? I'm at the Atlantic One right now, but I'm trying to find something more permanent for a month or two. Any ideas? Where are you staying?"

"I've got a room up the hill for $150 a month."

"Must not be much for that."

"Just a room and a bathroom."

"Oh. I'd like to get something with a kitchen, a one bedroom apartment, somewhere in the five to six hundred range."

"You're a big spender," Mitch said, smiling.

Even with Nels fatigue, the comment threw him. Five to six hundred monthly was the going rate for a one bedroom apartment and if you wanted long term the rate might be cheaper. This guy didn't know what he was talking about.

"What do you do for a living?" Nels asked.

"Oh, I do a lot of work with my computer and I'm an arms dealer."

If all you can afford is a $150 a month shithole, sales must not be that good, Nels thought.

"An arms dealer?" Nels asked, raising his eyebrow. "You serious?"

"Absolutely," Mitch said. "Let me know if you need a gun."

"Will do. Nice to meet you." Nels walked away thinking what a fuck-up Mitch was. Although, he had to admit, he had met many such people like him in Costambar. People who couldn't cut it in their home countries so they headed to the Caribbean to either hide out, or take what little money they had and stay for as long as they could. It didn't seem long before many of the them found themselves on the road to perdition and ended up drunk most of the time, walking around like a bunch of morally bankrupt zombies.

Nels hoped he wouldn't compromise his morality as he walked up the hill to the Atlantic One. He was beginning to feel a little drunk from the five or six beers he had consumed at the Catamaran. Certainly a nap was in order. Maybe call Novelee tomorrow.

Chapter Ten

3:32 pm, Sunday, December 18th, El Farolito Restaurant. Beachfront, Costambar.

"You sold your bed?" Nels asked Novelee in disbelief. Novelee had just finished telling him the story of how she had secured a one room apartment two months ago after her parents had kicked her out of their house for beating up her sister.

The whole thing didn't make sense to him as Novelee didn't have a job Even though he was told the rent was only two thousand pesos a month, how was she supposed to pay it without work? By selling her bed, he supposed. Next month, well she would deal with that when the time came.

"I had to sell my bed to pay the rent," Novelee said. "I owed November and December rent and the landlady started complaining to me yesterday when I got home. So I sold the bed for five thousand pesos and gave her four thousand."

"Can you believe it? I'm reduced to selling my bed? Life sucks."

He reclined in his beach chair staring out at the ocean waves, gently lapping up the sandy shoreline. *Better leave that one alone.* He had spent the morning looking for a monthly rental, and had finally ended up at a freshly painted six suite unit, about a block off the beach. He had run into a Canadian guy, Mel, earlier in the day and had been told about the unit. It was a one bedroom unit with a hard-wired internet connection, a newer TV and bed. The balcony overlooked the pool.

It needed a few repairs. Water was leaking from the bathroom ceiling and the hot water tank was fried. It had no accoutrements for cooking, but was equipped with a full kitchen. It seemed reasonably quiet by Dominican standards, but Nels had stayed in another building in roughly the same location previously and he knew from experience there were a few roosters living nearby that sounded off as early as 5:30 am. As well, there was a loud bar down the street that could get going quite late. And, he was sure the house next door, although well kept, was owned by a Dominican family. If they got going, particularly over the holidays, conversations and music could get loud-and last all night.

Mel also had a reputation for getting extremely drunk and crazy and hooking up with many hookers simultaneously. He lived in the suite above.

"I can get it ready for you by the 21st of December," Mel had said, smiling. He took a long pull on his Bohemia Grande. He was well on his way.

After some price negotiation, they settled at $600 from the 21st through to the end of January. Nels planned on finding a better apartment after that. So, he had paid Mel, received his receipt, and left the building wondering what the fuck he had just done.

He didn't have a good feeling about it. "What did you think of the suite?" he asked Novelee.

She looked at him and winced. "It's not very good at all."

"Why didn't you say something to me?"

"What, in front of the owner? What was I supposed to say?"

Nels sighed. She was right. Another fuck-up. He wondered why his judgement was often so impaired the first few weeks he arrived in the DR. It seemed, just as he was about to leave, he would figure things out.

He reached into his small knapsack, pulled out the large coke bottle of pre-mixed Cuba libre, pulled out two glasses and filled them both up, offering one to Novelee. "Salud," he said. They clinked glasses and smiled.

"I want to get wasted today," Novelee said. I'm pissed off about all the bad shit happening in my life."

Nels doubted the alcohol would do anything to rectify that but he took a long drink of his Cuba libre.

Two hours later, they sat on the Atlantic One balcony, tying into another bottle of rum, this time mixing it with a concoction of fruit juices. She talked. He listened.

"I don't know why you don't marry me," she said. Nels had heard this conversation before and through dulled senses he wondered why he had let Novelle get so drunk. With her thyroid condition, and a prescription that evidently was not working, alcohol was absolutely the last thing she needed.

The last time he had heard the conversation was when he had called her from Canada. Evidently she had been on a bit of a bender at the disco with another one of her sisters, probably the one she hadn't beaten to a pulp.

She had started ranting that he didn't love her enough to marry her, and pointedly questioning him about what his plans with her were. When you thought about it, Nels supposed, it was normal that a woman whom he had been with for three years, would start to wonder where the relationship was going.

But, when Novelee was drunk, she would beat the point to death.

"Honey, I love you, let's have this conversation when we're both sober," Nels said.

"You say you love me but why don't you prove it?" She made an unpleasant face.

He stood up from his plastic chair, went over and tried to kiss her on the cheek. She moved her face away. Nels knew better than to push the matter. He could end up with a slap in the face. He decided to change the subject.

"Are you hungry?" Food was always a good motivator for someone who would go days without meals when the money ran out.

"Yes, I am."

Thirty minutes later, they sat in a restaurant a couple blocks off the beach. Music thumped, tourists danced, and people played pool. Nels had recognized a few friends when they had entered, and had greeted them.

Now, he sat at a table with Novelee and she eyeballed the menu, which was in English. Nels translated very item for her and there wasn't a single thing she wanted. *For someone who is poverty-stricken, you sure are fussy*, he thought.

The waiter came. Nels ordered a bowl of chili with rice and Novelee ordered another beer. "She's fucking starving but can't find a single thing on the menu she likes. Go figure."

The waiter smiled, rolled his eyes, and took the menus. "Dominican women, you can't please them sometimes," he said before walking away.

Novelee couldn't understand English, but she could certainly pick up tones and expressions. She had noticed the waiter rolling his eyes and surmised quickly Nels had been talking badly about her.

Nels glanced over at her and she gave him the daggers. If looks could kill, he would be lying in a ditch somewhere.

A few moments later Nels' food arrived and he ate in silence.

"I know you said something bad about me to the waiter," Novelee said, eyeing the food hungrily.

"No, we were talking about something else," he lied. What was he supposed to say?

He offered her some food and she refused, turning her head away from him and staring around at the customers. He finished eating and took a pull of his beer.

"I think I'm going to order the bill," he told her.

"Why?" she asked.

"Do you think I enjoy sitting here all night getting the cold shoulder from you? I may as well go back to the apartment and sleep."

Her demeanor changed and she leaned over and kissed him. "Can I order some of that?" she asked.

"Sure," he said, approaching the busy bar to get the waiter's attention. "My girlfriend wants the chili and rice please."

"Sorry, we're out of that. Would you like me to send over our cook to explain what sort of combinations can be created?"

"Sure," Nels said. "It's worth a try."

The cook came over to their table. After a lengthy explanation, Novelee finally decided on a grilled cheese sandwich.

A few minutes later it arrived and she looked at it with disgust-like she had never seen a grilled cheese sandwich before in her life.

She picked it up, took a small bite, and began spewing small globs of cheese sandwich and vomit on the floor. The place was crowded and Nels thought nobody noticed. But he was also wasted,; so how acute were his senses?

Novelee got up from the table and ran into the bathroom. About five minutes later she returned, saying she wouldn't eat the sandwich, that it was disgusting. It looked fine to Nels, but he wasn't about to try it after watching her throw up.

It was time to leave.

Nels paid the bill and the two staggered out. They only had about five blocks to return to Atlantic One, but some streets were without streetlights, and lined with a canopy of trees that obscured the moonlight and made visibility difficult.

Nels' night vision wasn't great at the best of times.

They rounded a corner and couldn't see a thing in front of them. Novelee complained she was scared, and picked up her pace.

Suddenly barking dogs could be heard, the sounds coming closer.

Novelee had always been petrified of stray dogs-and particularly barking ones.

Nels could faintly make out Novelee's shape ahead of him. "Don't run," he said. "You'll just encourage them."

"I'm scared."

Now the dogs were at Nels' heals, barking louder. He could feel hot breath on his bare ankles and felt he would get bitten soon.

He remembered something an ex-pat friend had told him once and he bent down swiftly in a motion that approximated picking up a rock. He picked up nothing and made a throwing motion.

The dogs scattered, the barks grew faint. Dominican dogs were used to people throwing rocks at them.

Nels caught up to Novelee, put his arm around her, and in a few minutes they arrived at the apartment. Novelee's moods had been swinging like a rollercoaster all day and he thought the best thing to do was to go to sleep.

She sensed his reluctance to engage in any intimacy with her, walked into the bedroom, found an extra pillow and small blanket and returned to the living room, curling up on the small loveseat.

In his bedroom, Nels looked at a Zoplicone pill and contemplated taking it. They seemed to work well with alcohol. He realized he was drunk enough to pass out, so put the pill back on the nightstand.

As he drifted off, there was one lingering thought in his mind.

End his relationship with Novelee-permanently.

Chapter Eleven

10:55 am, Monday, December 19th. Atlantic One, Costambar.

Nels woke with a pounding headache. Novelee wasn't looking particularly spry either. He had heard her phone ring a few times earlier and finally decided to get up. He hadn't heard a single rooster in the morning and was thankful the complex was strategically located-out of earshot of all the roosters. Evidently, this barrio was not their stomping grounds.

"Good morning," he said, trying to muster a smile.

"Good morning," she answered with a weak smile.

"How did you sleep?" he asked.

"Okay, but I woke up a few times in the middle of the night."

"Yeah, me too. Who keeps calling?"

"Oh it's that girl I'm supposed to hook up with your friend. I keep telling her I'll call when he arrives but she won't take no for an answer."

Nels had had second thoughts about the whole thing. It didn't sit well with him anymore. He had told Novelee previously Wilson was coming but he had yet to confirm an arrival date. Of course, he now had an arrival date but Nels wasn't sure he wanted to proceed.

They had some instant coffee, showered, dressed and left the apartment. Nels had mentioned to Novelee he would give her two thousand pesos for some food and send her home. He wanted to spend the whole day working, undisturbed.

They walked down the street together toward the gates of Costambar. Nels accompanied her as he had a few items to pick up at the supermarket. As they walked, he saw a Dominican man driving a motoconcho with one hand, and in the other he held two, twenty-foot steel bars. They dragged along the road behind him, sparking as they rattled against the pavement.

Nels wondered if the rods were to be used for construction, what would the structural integrity be like after they reached the destination? Probably not that good.

Another motoconcho passed him. The driver talked on his cell phone, animated.

Still another motoconcho drove past, the driver drinking a Bohemia Grande. Bohemia fog. Nels had been told drunk drivers came out in droves during Christmas and New Year's. It was absolutely the worst and most dangerous time to be on the road in the DR. He had deliberately brought with him enough money so he would not have to go to the Scotia bank in Puerto Plata until at least January 3rd, 2012, by which time most of the drunk drivers would be recovering.

Or dead.

Nels shook his head and continued.

They arrived at the supermarket and Novelee accompanied him inside. He bought a few toiletry items, a few Bohemia Grande beers, and a 250 peso phone card.

They exited the store and he asked Novelee to input the minutes into the phone. They sat on a bench outside the store next to a fat man drinking a beer and she pressed a number combination on his phone, loading the minutes.

He thanked her, kissed her on the lips, handed her two thousand pesos, and watched her walk toward the gates.

He knew his timing could be better. He was dumping her at one of her worst moments-psychologically, financially and physically. And, of course, Christmas was just around the corner.

But, at that point in time, Nels sincerely hoped he would never see Novelee again for the rest of his life.

Chapter Twelve

11:30 am, Monday, December 19th, Cabarete, North Coast, Dominican Republic.

Julie sat in the kitchen of her beachfront house and poured the cooked stews into separate plastic containers. At 67, she and her husband Robert had retired and had bought a small house in this popular beachfront community. She had worked as a school teacher and her husband was an electrical engineer. They were both from Toronto, Ontario, Canada.

When she did cook, Julie liked to prepare a lot of meals in advance. She was organized and did not like slaving over a hot stove in the Caribbean heat every day. It was their second year into retirement, and so far their life had been idyllic.

For something to do, they had opened up a small store in the town, were involved in community service work, and Robert often helped build houses for the homeless. And there were many who needed help.

She was looking forward to freezing all the prepared stews so they could spend a peaceful and relaxing day at the beach, a few steps from their backyard.

Robert busied himself in the garden, raking out weeds from the many vegetables they were growing.

He heard a rustling sound behind him and turned, lifting the rake up as he did.

Eduardo interpreted the gesture as a threat and pulled the trigger on his handgun. A single bullet penetrated Robert's head, right between the eyes. He had time to gasp and utter a small scream, before falling with a thud, the rake landing on top of him.

Julie heard the crack of the pistol, glanced out the sliding glass doors and saw her husband drop. She panicked and ran outside. In retrospect, she thought she would have been better off to leave from the front door, which would have put more distance between her and the killer.

But the shock of seeing her husband gasp, scream and die in front of her had been too much.

Eduardo was behind her in no time. He fired a shot that narrowly missed her and ordered her to stop or die.

She froze to the spot.

He grabbed her aggressively, hauling her into the house, where he threw her into a chair and quickly bound her legs and arms with some zip straps he was carrying.

"Where's the money?" he demanded.

"What I have is in the bedroom safe," Julie said, her face turning an ashen grey, matching the creases in her face and her short-cropped grey hair.

"What's the combination?" Eduardo asked, leveling the pistol at her head.

Julie winced. She couldn't remember it.

"What's the combination?" Eduardo asked again, walking closer and pressing the barrel of the gun into her forehead.

She felt the hot steel on her forehead. Then it came to her. "It's 4368," she said.

"Where is the safe exactly?" he said, his eyes narrowing.

"In the bedroom closet, in the wall behind the clothes."

"You better be right," he said, tearing a strip of cloth from one of the window coverings and wrapping it tightly around her mouth.

"Make a sound and I'll kill you," he said, walking from the kitchen into the bedroom.

While he was gone, Julie struggled, trying to free her arms. It was no use. One of the plastic zip ties on her wrist was so tight it was cutting off circulation to her hand. She watched her hand turn blue and realized struggling only made it worse.

Eduardo returned with two Canadian passports, two credit cards, a bank card and two thousand pesos. "You think you're going to get rid of me with this," he said, throwing the contents on the kitchen table.

He wacked her in the side of the head with the butt of his revolver and smiled. She uttered a muffled scream and her eyes widened. A small cut opened above her right eye and blood trickled into it. She pointed her finger toward her cloth gag, motioning for him to remove it.

Eduardo look at her blankly.

She pointed her finger again, uttering some muffled words.

Her understood one of them and removed the gag.

Julie took a deep breath while Eduardo stared at her.

"Where is the rest of your money?" he asked, stuffing the barrel of the gun inside her mouth.

Julie gagged and spit on her red and white flowery dress as he removed the gun. "It's in my store," she said.

"What store? Where?"

"I own a small supermarket two blocks from here. We can go there if you like, in my car. I'll get you more money. I have sixty thousand pesos there."

Eduardo smiled, thinking he could do a lot with sixty thousand pesos. He set the gun on the kitchen table, scratched his head and wondered how he could get away with getting his hands on the money in broad daylight without getting caught.

He thought of calling Fabiola, get her to pick up the money, but thought better of it. He had an idea. Julie could call the store, tell one of her employees to bring the money out to her vehicle, while he held her at gunpoint in the backseat.

He cycled the idea through his limited mind a few times and realized it might work. He knew Julie's SUV had tinted glass, and if he was pointing the gun at the back of her head from the back seat, he just might get away with it.

The only problem would be if someone spotted him. Then he would have to kill Julie and the witness, and risk being seen by more people as he made his getaway.

On the other hand, what if she was lying? What if there was more money in the house? But, after seeing her husband die in front of her, would this woman risk being killed over sixty thousand pesos. He studied the fear in her eyes and doubted it.

What the hell. A little more interrogating wouldn't hurt.

"Where is the rest of the money in your house?" he asked, raising the butt of the revolver high over her head.

"I told you, I don't have any more money here. It's in the store. Take me there and I'll have Angie bring it out to you."

An hour later, Julie, white knuckled, pulled her green SUV in front of her store and speed-dialed Angie from her cell.

Eduardo sat in the back seat, gun pointed at the back of her head.

He had turned the house contents upside down before leaving, just to be sure. He had the cash, cards and passports in his back pocket. He had found nothing else of value.

Angie had detected the fear in her boss's voice and her hands trembled as she walked to the vehicle. Julie lowered the window, slightly, just enough to receive the cash. The street was busy with vehicular and pedestrian traffic.

Jim, an ex-pat friend, was walking down the street and recognized the green SUV. "What's with all the cloak and dagger stuff?" the 70 year old pot-bellied bald man asked, as he wrenched open the driver door, just after Angie had handed Julie the bag of money through the small opening in the window.

Eduardo's eyes met Jim's and he froze. He knew the man, had talked to him on the beach, trying to bait him into a planned robbery involving the sexually desirable Fabiola.

There were way too many people around to start firing bullets. *Why did I make this plan?* Eduardo asked himself as he grabbed the paper bag from Julie's trembling hands, opened the door, darted from the vehicle and disappeared.

Julie slumped in the driver's seat as cars began honking horns. Her heart pounded so fast she could hear its thumping. She thought she was going to have a heart attack.

Chapter Thirteen

11:56 pm, Thursday, December 22nd, Small one room apartment in seedy, impoverished neighborhood, on the hill, Puerto Plata.

Novelee walked down the public hallway leading to the door of her run down one room apartment, her young son Papito in tow. She noticed some splintered wood on the hallway floor and her eyes followed the wood trail to her door, which was ajar and dangling precariously on one hinge.

Her eyes widened in shock as she realized she had been broken into and robbed. What little possessions she had, including her son's clothing, had been stolen. Everything was gone, including what little toiletries and make-up she possessed.

Even her son's school uniform had been stolen, which meant he would not be able to attend school any longer.

She had spent the day down the street at her parent's three bedroom apartment, doing the laundry for her mother. Lately, her mother's stools were red with blood and she didn't have much energy. For the last three days, her mother had slept most of the day and night, only getting up to eat a few things and use the bathroom. She didn't have the money to get her condition diagnosed as her husband had just been laid off from his job as a security guard for one of the five star hotels in Playa Dorada. The closure of the hotel due to dwindling tourist attendance had meant the end of his employment.

Novelee had tried calling Nels about twelve times that day and had not been able to reach him. He would not answer his phone.

She crumpled onto the makeshift bed her landlady had donated to her after she had sold her new one to pay the rent. The springs of the old mattress jutted out and she curled up uncomfortably and sobbed.

Papito laid down beside his mother and put his small arm around her slender body as she convulsed. He put his head to her breast and listened to her heart. It was racing.

Chapter Fourteen

11:56 pm, Friday, December 23. Nels' one bedroom apartment. One block from beach, Costambar.

Nels lay on his comfortable queen-sized bed and put the earplugs back in.

He had been drinking all day on the beach and had staggered back to his apartment to try and get some shut-eye.

Even with the earplugs, he could hear Bachata music thumping out from a nearby bar. Drunken Dominicans in the house next door talked and shouted loudly. Nels could no longer tell if they were happy or arguing. But he knew one thing. The decibel level had increased since he had arrived at his apartment two hours ago.

He had moved into his new apartment two days ago and slowly but surely things had started to break down. On the second day he moved in he noticed his room number.

Four.

First, the hot water tank went.

Next, water started pouring out from the bathroom ceiling. Nels didn't know if it was sewage or tap water but the bathroom now had two inches of water, and was beginning to flow out and into the hallway.

Then the fridge started rattling every three or so minutes. It sounded like the burst of machine gun fire, but the old clunker wouldn't quit. Just as Nels was about to drift off, the fridge would rat-a-tat-tat and he would stir and turn over in his sleep.

He hadn't been having any nightmares lately because he was barely able to sleep.

So, today he had gotten himself wasted, thinking he would just pass-out. At least then he would get some down-time, albeit alcohol-induced.

Walking around in a fog for the last two days, he had been barely able to get any work done. He had answered mandatory emails regarding his rental properties, and fired off a short article for some website content he was writing for a client. The client had suggested some edits and so far Nels hadn't gone near the 1,500 word piece of work.

He was afraid he would fuck it up.

He had received many calls from Novelee but so far his resolve had held. He had not picked up the phone. If he had to be completely honest with himself, however, his determination was fading and he was starting to wonder how she was doing.

He couldn't shake the sense she was in some kind of trouble. And, he had gone back on his word, he remembered. He had told her he would pay for another doctor visit to start her on a new prescription, and a new vitamin regiment. He couldn't help but notice how gaunt she had looked the last time he had seen her.

And he also thought he had been too quick to judge her, not giving her the benefit of the doubt regarding her thyroid condition. Since her departure a few days ago, he had called a few of his friends regarding a thyroid problem and had learned it could cause all kinds of personality disorders.

Nels was thinking of Novelee when a loud intermittent beeping sound snapped him out of his contemplation.

He staggered into the kitchen, trying to determine the source. It was the inverter, back-up battery power supply used to power a few outlets during the many power outages. Ask ten people why the power went out so frequently in the DR and you would get ten different answers. Nels had given up trying to solve the conundrum.

He looked at the inverter beeping loudly, every second or so, and had no idea what to do about it. He had no power whatsoever. *That's it. Tomorrow I'm getting the hell out of this rat-hole.*

He dug out two sleeping pills from his end table drawer in the bedroom, poured a glass of water, and chased them down, draining the glass.

Chapter Fifteen

1:33 pm, Saturday, December 24, Catamaran Restaurant, Beachfront, Costambar.

"How many dead inside of a month?" Nels asked Tim after finishing his lunch and ordering his fourth beer.

"Three," Tim said.

He was a beefy man with clear blue eyes and a thick patch of grey hair on the sides of his head. The middle of his head was bald. He was 56, a semi-retired oil worker from Edmonton, Alberta. He spent about six months of the year in the DR, and from what Nels had been able to gather, went on a charity mission helping his girlfriend, her family, and even relatives, doling out lots of cash in the process.

Nels' mind had been drifting when Tim suddenly said three deaths. In a moment of sagacity, he had looked at the man sitting across from him with shock.

"What happened?" Nels asked, gulping the beer the waitress had put on his table.

"Well first my girlfriend of three years got parasites in her stomach. It was misdiagnosed initially, and by the time they got the diagnosis right the parasites had spread to her brain and it was too late."

"Sorry to hear that," Nels said.

"Then my girlfriend's brother and sister got wasted on rum and decided it would be a good idea to race each other on motoconchos."

"Race each other? Was it at night?"

"Yeah. Anyway, they crashed during the race. She's still alive and he died in the crash."

"Wow. That's awful."

"It gets worse. My girlfriend's grandmother gets gangrene, they cut off two toes. Not good enough. It spreads. They cut off her foot. It spreads again. They cut off her leg below the knee. It spreads again and she dies about a week later."

"Shit, what are you going to do now," Nels asked looking out at the waves gently lapping against the shore, and enjoying the gentle breeze blowing through the oasis of plants sheltering the seating area from the brunt of the wind.

"I'm thinking of buying the grandmother's house so the family has a place to live. They don't have much money."

"That's awfully big of you."

"I just like helping people."

Twenty minutes later, Nels walked up the beach, toward his new apartment. Through some ex-pat connections, he had lined up some new digs at 9:30 am that morning. He had talked to the Canadian owner of the cursed building at 11:30 am, explaining that everything in the unit was falling apart and he hadn't signed up for this.

To his credit, the owner gave Nels a portion of the rent back, saying "I don't want to be the bad guy in all this."

In any event, the inverter was fried and, with Christmas, it would be at least four days before Nels would have any power or internet, and who knew how long it would take to repair the other problems.

He walked along the shore line, looking out at the ocean and daydreaming. He looked at the restaurants, watching the patrons laugh, talk, eat and drink. He remembered something an ex-pat had told him a few years back in the DR. She claimed to have spent about 10 million pesos helping Dominican poor people and they were, for the most part, unappreciative.

"Hey you," Mitch said, staggering up to him, a half full Presidente Grande in his left hand.

Nels was surprised he remembered the name. "Mitch, how you doing?"

Mitch was out of his tree. "Great," Mitch said, giving Nels a creepy look and a crooked smile. "I've been walking all around Costambar all day and decided to stop for a beer. Want to join me."

"No, I'm moving into my new apartment today. It's supposed to be ready now."

"Oh," Mitch said, through glazed eyes. "What city are you from?"

"Calgary."

"Right, did I tell you I was born in Calgary?"

"Yeah, last time we talked."

"Oh."

"What have you been up to lately?"

"I've been working a lot, selling guns and knives over the phone in my room. I make about a thousand dollars a week and all I do is talk."

"How long you down here for?"

"Forever."

"Oh. You left your apartment in the States?"

"I never had an apartment in the States."

"Didn't you say you were living there before coming here?"

"Yeah, but I'm a nomad, like my dad. I don't stay in any place for longer than a few months. Then I move on."

"Have you ever been to Jakarta?" Mitch asked.

"No."

"I'd like to go there but I don't know what it's like."

"Only one way to find out," Nels said.

"That's right. Go there. Do you know I've been in every city in the world?"

"Ever been to Manilla?"

"Can't say as I have. Hey do you know where I can find a decent apartment?"

Nels wanted no part of trying to help this fuck-up. Who knew where it might lead. "It's pretty full here right now. But ask around. Don't you like your place anymore?"

"No, I don't have a kitchen. But my neighbors cook for me. And they let me put valuables and stuff in their house next door. There's no security in my building."

"So you go over and eat with them?"

"Yeah."

"How much does that cost?"

"I give them ten thousand pesos a week. They have enough food in their house to feed all of Costambar. Want to have a look at my place?"

"No, I have to go."

"You know the only problem with it?"

"What's that?" Nels asked, many problems coming to mind.

"Well I went there this afternoon and nobody answers the door. My stuff is inside and they won't answer the door."

"You'd be better off to rent a furnished apartment with a kitchen for six hundred or so a month. Do the math. You're giving the family $1,080 a month, plus paying $150 a month for your room. Now you can't get into their unit to get your stuff, or eat for that matter."

A Dominican girl walked up behind Mitch and circled her head with her index finger, pointing at him. Nels gave her a telling glance and she walked away.

"I think I'm trapped there," Mitch said. "If I try to leave they might get pissed off at me, keep my stuff. Want to see the place?"

Nels cell phone rang. He looked at the number. It was Novelee.

"Excuse me," he said, walking away. "I have to go now. See you around." Hoping that he wouldn't.

Chapter Sixteen

Nels looked down at Novelee on the hospital bed, breathing erratically with an oxygen mask strapped to her face.

A doctor stood beside him with a chart, monitoring her condition.

Novelee's sister Esmerelda, sat beside Novelee holding her hand and crying.

Novelee smiled at Nels. He smiled back. "I'm sorry," he said. "My mind has been preoccupied with problems."

"Mine too," she said, smiling weakly.

"It's four thousand pesos," the doctor told Nels.

He dug into one of the many zippered pockets of his travel pants and counted out the money. "Here," he said, handing it to the doctor.

When he had answered the cell phone on the beach, it was Esmerelda on the other end. She had told him about Novelee being in the hospital and asked for four thousand pesos. After settling into his new apartment, a 1,200 square foot two bedroom unit with a peek-a-boo ocean view, that needed many upgrades, but also looked to be very peaceful, he had called his trusty motoconcho driver Daniel and was on his way to the hospital.

The doctor took the money and escorted him outside into the hallway. "She arrived here last night, sobbing, complaining of shortness of breath. Her heart was beating incredibly fast, and we don't really know what caused it. We don't know if it's related to the thyroid problem, but we've started her on a new prescription and a new vitamin regiment. Are you her boyfriend?"

Nels nodded. He didn't know what else to do.

"We're going to release her tomorrow, but we eventually want to x-ray her throat to try and understand why she keeps having pain there."

"Can I stay with her for awhile?"

"A little while but not too long. She needs to rest right now. She hasn't been sleeping a lot. She says you dumped her and stopped returning her calls and her apartment was recently broken into and robbed. She says all that started her downward spiral."

Nels felt like a piece of shit. So, he just nodded and returned to Novelee's room as the doctor turned and walked down the hall.

He sat down in an empty chair beside the bed, put his hand on her arm. Her sister still sat at the other side of the bed but had stopped crying.

"Merry Christmas," he said and immediately felt stupid.

"Same to you," she squeaked through the oxygen mask.

He bent down and kissed her on the cheek. "I'm sorry," he said. "Things were becoming way too problematic for me. I got scared and confused."

"It's okay," Novelee said. "Are you back?"

"Yes I am. Are you still living in the apartment? The doctor told me."

"No, I moved in with my cousin, her husband and baby daughter. My son and I are sleeping on the floor."

"Sorry to hear that."

"Me too. I know I have to stop thinking about the robbery but it still occupies my mind a lot. Papito's school uniform was stolen. He can't go to school now."

"I'll buy him a school uniform."

"Thank you."

Esmerelda watched the exchange with interest and Nels suddenly realized he hadn't been formally introduced. He walked to her side of the bed, introduced himself, and kissed the air beside her cheek.

She did the same and smiled at him, searching him with her stunning brown eyes. She had short cropped brown hair, a nice smile, olive-toned skin and gentle features. She was attractive, just falling short of being beautiful.

Nels was tired and he wanted to go home to his new apartment. After the hellish experience in the first apartment, he was hoping this one would be better. He told her he would call her tomorrow and visit her at her family's home for Christmas. He knew that probably meant buying all the groceries but he didn't give a shit anymore.

Right now, he wanted a less complicated and healthy life. And he wanted a good night's sleep, with no nightmares.

Wasn't he supposed to be on vacation?

Chapter Seventeen

10:55 am, Sunday, December 25th, Christmas Day. Nels' new apartment, Costambar.

Nels had had a fitful night. He had slept a little, but found himself waking up every hour, walking out to the peaceful balcony of his apartment, and then returning to bed.

He even had a short nightmare that he remembered clearly. He was in his Chevy Trailblazer with a couple of friends. He was in the back trying to sleep while they drove around a Calgary neighborhood looking at houses. The seats were folded back and he had fashioned a bed with a small blanket and a pillow.

Arriving at a house they supposedly liked, the couple exited the vehicle and started looking at the property. The female owner came by and asked them what they were doing, to which they replied they were interested in buying it.

After some discussion, of which the details were unclear, his friends left. He walked behind them for a time. They rounded a corner and disappeared from sight.

Nels returned to his vehicle and discovered it was missing. Additionally he did not have his cell phone and he suddenly had no idea where he was. Convinced it was a nightmare, he had tried to wake himself.

But, again he couldn't.

So he wandered around the streets and finally decided to knock on the door of a house to ask for help. After all, he didn't have a phone or a dime in his pocket.

Three beautiful women answered the door and he asked if he could come in and use a phone.

A stunning young blonde of about 25 eyed him through her spectacles and finally decided he was harmless.

"Come in," she had said. "But you can't stay long."

"No, I just want to make a call," he had replied.

"You only have one call," the blonde had said, eyeing him seriously.

He stood at the entrance while one of the women returned with a cordless phone.

Meanwhile, he could see another one undressing in the open concept living room and he was treated to a nice view of her perky breasts as she pulled off her top.

He looked at the phone and knew exactly who he was going to call. He even had the number committed to memory.

Belinda. He would call her and she would bail him out.

Then, he had woken up. Everything in the dream was crystal clear and he sat on his balcony drinking coffee and looking around, trying to determine the meaning.

Nothing came to him and he eyed his surroundings. He loved the ocean view and at night the wind and waves whistled through the slat like windows, blowing the tan blinds in all different directions. It was nothing fancy, and by real estate standards would be considered a fixer upper at best.

But the location was awesome and very peaceful for Costambar. Nels had not heard a single dog bark or a single rooster when he had woken up. The unit had two bedrooms and two bathrooms. One of the bathrooms was closed and the Dominican owner Juan had told Nels it needed repairs and was therefore off limits.

Juan, a pleasant and muscular ex-military soldier and ex-cop, kept a close guard on the premises, making sure his tenants were happy and safe. Nels and him had instantly hit it off and now Juan referred to Nels as his brother, smiling every time he saw him. Juan was always armed with a pistol and he had a couple of larger guns in his suite above Nels, where he lived with his girlfriend, Oria. He had told Nels when he moved in that if anyone ever bothered him, he was available to help.

Just a phone call away.

He had even bought an internet cable and had hard-wired Nels' suite, the cable running right down the stairs from Juan's suite and right into his front door, along the floor and into the computer, on the kitchen table.

Sure, the bathroom toilet leaked a bit, the bathroom tap had a steady drip, the kitchen needed a complete overhaul, there was just barely enough accoutrements to cook, and some of the windows were missing screens, but Nels had felt a positive energy from the minute he walked in the door.

It was just a vibe.

The concrete white building contained six suites, had a nice swimming pool, which few tenants used, and was less than a block to the beach.

Another thing he thought would bother him. But it didn't.

The suite number.

Four.

He looked out at the ocean, felt the warm breeze, heard the ocean waves and wind and smiled as he took in the blue sky dotted with a few clouds. The high was forecast to be 28 degrees Celsius, the low, a balmy 23 degrees.

"I'm in the Caribbean," he said to himself, picking up his phone to call Novelee.

Chapter Eighteen

3:20 pm, Sunday, December 25th, three bedroom apartment, seedy area of Puerto Plata.

Nels arrived at Novelee's home via his motoconcho driver, Daniel. Many of the streets going through the poor barrio were made of large, loose boulders and there were potholes galore. People had tables and chairs set up curbside and played dominoes and cards. Kids played in the streets and motoconchos zipped around, creating a steady hum of noise pollution. Add to that the dogs barking, music thumping from boom boxes, the drunks carrying on and the neighborhood had a disconcerting edge to it.

If you let it get to you.

Which Nels did not as Daniel expertly weaved his way to the destination.

One thing Nels did notice; a distinct absence of gringos. Many people, including some attractive Dominican females, stared at him as he passed them on the streets.

He pulled in front of the apartment, a faded concrete yellowish building, the entrance-way consisting of odd sized gravel and dirt-one of the first signs of how impoverished things around here were.

Nels walked up the stairs and the family greeted him.

He kissed and hugged Novelee, and hugged the rest of the family.

The father, Jesus, was a small man of about five foot five, about 55 years old, grey hair, inquisitive eyes and an easy smile.

Jeanette, the mother was about the same height and the same age and also smiled easily. She had plain, but friendly and honest features. And she loved to joke around.

And little Papito.

And the sister, Esmeralda.

Novelee's brother Carlos lived in Barbaro and was absent from the ceremony.

Novelee's sister Gloria, perhaps still recovering from her recent beatings, was also absent.

It quickly became evident there was an absence of food and beer, so Novelee and Nels walked up the street to a small store and purchased two chickens, rice, beans, some candy for Papito, some cooking oil, an assortment of fruit and cookies for desert.

Oh, and of course a dozen large Bohemias and a bottle of Brugal, Anejo dark rum.

Nels sat in one of four rocking chairs around a small table and some of the family sat around him and stared.

The women worked in the kitchen while Nels struck up a conversation with Jesus about the troubled economy in the DR, and how difficult it was too find work. Nels had read recently in one of the local papers that the DR had one of the lowest monthly salaries in the Caribbean, at around $260.00 US per month.

He noticed the windows had no screens, but the 1,100 square foot three bedroom unit was kept very clean. The couches in the living room looked new. They were loaded with cushions and it appeared they were rarely used.

When he went to the bathroom, he discovered there was no door handle and none of the plumbing worked. He wasn't able to flush the toilet.

He also noticed as he sat down his ankles were getting red with mosquito bites.

On a few occasions, Novelee came into the living room to discipline Papito, sometimes slapping him firmly on the head and arms. This was followed by shouting and nasty glares that Nels wished he would not be on the other end of any time soon. The kid actually seemed fairly well behaved and Nels figured without education it was the only way Novelee knew how to raise her son. Maybe she had been raised the same way?

Perhaps she resented the deadbeat father and took it out on the son. Maybe, just looking at him reminded her of how much she hated his father.

He couldn't help but think that if he wanted a charity case it was right here in front of him. He didn't have to volunteer for an orphanage, build houses for the poor, or donate money to the many charities operating in the DR.

All he had to do was help this family. Novelee had mentioned to him earlier the family hadn't eaten for three days. They just didn't have the money.

He was feeling numb from the alcohol. Maybe that was the only way he could handle this poverty.

As they wolfed the food down, he asked Novelee, who was also filling her mouth with huge portions of rice, beans, and chicken, a question: "If you could have five things in your life what would they be?"

Her mouth was overflowing with food. She chewed it down, took a drink of water and looked at him in surprise. Nels doubted if she would give him the lecture regarding eating and not talking.

Surely not on Christmas day.

And not in front of her family.

"What about you?" she said.

"I asked you first."

"I asked you second."

"Okay, fine," Nels said.

He took a sip of his beer, put down his fork, while the entire family stared at him.

"Five things, okay. One, I would like to develop true inner peace. Two, I would like to write a best-selling novel. Three, I would like to continue to grow and develop as a person, become better. Four, I would like to put myself in a position where I could help people better their lives. Five, I want lots of love in my life from friends and family."

There was a long silence as the family pondered this.

"Your turn," Nels said, before Novelee could shovel a large spoonful of beans and rice into her mouth.

"Okay," she said, putting the spoon down, probably a first for her.

Number one, I would like to have my thyroid problem fixed. I don't want to die. Two, I would like to have my own business doing nails and feet. Three, I would like to have a house of my own to live in. Four, I would like lots of love in my life. Five, I would like to change the way I respond to situations."

Nels was pleasantly surprised at the five things. Although to some people they might sound selfish, after all she hadn't mentioned bettering the life of her kid or family, she had seemed to recognize that there were probably better ways to deal with disagreements with her sister than thumping the shit out of her.

Chapter Nineteen

2:55 pm, Saturday, December 31, Nels' apartment, one block from beach, Costambar.

"I'll order some more beer from Yenny's," Nels said to the group sitting poolside.

Fabiola, Novelee, Wilson and Jonas sat on green plastic chairs at a green plastic table with a green umbrella. They had started drinking about one in the afternoon and were running out of beer.

It was hot outside but a gentle breeze blew in from the ocean. They were getting pleasantly drunk in preparation for their New Year's Eve party at El Farolito Restaurant, beachside.

"You can do that?" Wilson asked.

"Yeah, but you have to be able to speak Spanish." Which Nels knew, Wilson could not.

Nels picked up his phone and ordered twelve large Bohemias and some toilet paper. It seemed he always needed toilet paper.

"I'll give you some money," Wilson offered. His blue eyes were a little glazed and he had a smile on his face. He was about five foot six, a slim 180 pounds, with short-cropped greyish black hair. He had an easy smile and very good people skills. Which had helped make him a successful real estate developer. It didn't hurt that he was well connected with money people in Calgary.

"I got it," Nels said, putting down his phone. He had consumed a lot, but didn't feel drunk. He had spent the last few days nightmare-free and had even slept reasonably well-a rarity for him this early in a trip. It usually took him three weeks to a month to begin to adjust to a third world culture.

Before leaving Novelee's parents, he had given her four thousand pesos for some clothing and food, and had left her alone for a few days to regroup. According to Novelee, the new prescription was helping somewhat, but she was still feeling some pain in her throat and was worried she was going to die.

Nels wasn't sure what to make of Fabiola. His initial impression was good but that had slowly changed as he got to know her a little. She seemed to converse little, and offered short answers when questioned.

Of course not knowing Spanish, Wilson's discourse with her was extremely limited. Nels and Jonas had done some translation, and they were trying to figure out if he liked her.

"What do you think of her?" Jonas asked Wilson. Jonas had short, cropped brown hair, clear blue eyes, a pleasant smile and wasn't bad looking in his own right. His sharp mind was always analyzing things and he was a well-seasoned traveler who could think quickly on his feet and navigate his way through stormy waters. He had gotten himself out of some tight situations with hookers on many occasions in the Sewer.

Jonas and Wilson had become fast friends.

"I don't know if I like braces," Wilson said.

"Yeah but she's got big tits," Nels said. But Nels was the tit man-not Wilson. He was an ass man. And, while Fabiola's ass was a little plump, it was still quite shapely.

"Give me a little more time and another beer," Wilson said.

Nels cracked the cap from the Bohemia Grande and filled up his glass.

Jonas talked of his exploits in Spain. "I remember booking a hotel room and I was a little drunk at the time. Well, I checked in and went right out to another bar, met some people and started drinking some more. One thing led to another and at about three in the morning. I started trying to find my room and had no idea where it was. I was too drunk. I remember knocking on a few doors and being greeting by some rather angry Spaniards."

"Finally, I thought I arrived at my building. Well, the gate was locked and, too drunk to realize I had a key, I started banging on the big steel door to the complex. Finally the manager came and let me in, berating me the entire time while I staggered to my room."

Wilson and Nels laughed. The girls didn't have a clue what Jonas was saying. He had told the story in English.

It was Nels' turn. "I remember visiting Amsterdam, going into a bar after I checked into a hotel. I got to know some of the locals well, probably my Dutch heritage and all, and they closed the bar to the public at about one in the morning. Needless to say, I stayed and drank with them until about six in the morning. Although my hotel was just down the street from the bar, maybe four buildings away, I must've walked around the block six times before I finally found it. And, man, was I hurting the next day."

Wilson and Jonas laughed and the girls looked confused.

"I remember getting so wasted in Turkey one time I stood outside my hotel room for an hour trying to find my key. Meanwhile I was holding it in my hand," Wilson said.

Jonas' phone suddenly rang. "You deal with it," he said, handing it to Nels. "It's one of the girls I was with in Sosua. All she did was watch Spanish novellas when she came over and she thinks I'm interested in her. She phones a lot."

Nels grabbed the phone.

"Hello," he said, trying to fake a Swedish accent while speaking Spanish. "How are you?" She gave a quick response and Nels continued. "Listen, I am with some friends now and have a meeting tomorrow, which means I'll be unavailable for two days. I'll be in touch after that. Is that okay?"

The woman said yes, so Nels hung up.

"There," he said, handing the phone to Jonas. "I just bought you two days."

"Thanks," Jonas said, and smiled.

Four hours later they sat at El Farolito Restaurant and Bar drinking, waiting for their New Year's Eve dinner, laughing and joking.

The restaurant was full of patrons enjoying themselves. Heaps of wood were piled up on the beach in the shape of a teepee, for what would later become a giant bonfire on the beach. From that strategic point, they would also be able to watch the midnight fireworks display from nearby Cofressi.

Eduardo watched from behind a nearby tree. He extracted his long knife, ran his forefinger along the blade. Satisfied it was sharp enough, he slid it back into its leather holder fastened to his belt. He pulled out the revolver, checked the safety. It was off, just how he liked it.

He had shaved his head bald, and was beginning to grow a goatee, an attempt at disguising himself. He was a wanted man.

By fifteen minutes to midnight, they had all enjoyed a huge buffet meal. Everything tasted awesome, and the conversation slowed while they digested their food. Novelee had promptly fallen asleep after eating. Her head was tilted back, her mouth open and she snored occasionally.

A few of the patrons looked at her and laughed. Even Nels found it funny, but didn't bother to wake her. He knew she had been having trouble sleeping lately due to her thyroid condition and he felt if she was finally sleeping, she probably needed it.

Fabiola excused herself to go to the bathroom. She had been rather quiet all night and Nels found it disturbing. He didn't trust her.

At the bathroom, her phone rang. It was Eduardo. "Get him to the room now. I think I've been made. I can't hang around here too long."

"Okay," she said and hung up.

Seated back at the table, she put her hand on Wilson's knee and he responded with a smile. "Let's go back to your room," she said.

He looked at her blankly. "What's she saying?

Nels asked her to repeat it.

"I want to take him back to his room for a few hours, because my Mother who it babysitting my kid can only do it until two in the morning," she said.

Jonas raised his eyebrows. "That sounds like she's making it up."

"What?" Wilson asked.

"She says she wants to go to your room for a few hours as her mother's babysitting shift ends at two in the morning, and she can't stay all night," Nels said.

"That doesn't make any sense," Wilson said. "It's just before midnight anyway. We have to see in 2012."

"Absolutely," Nels said. "I'm not going anywhere until after midnight, then it'll probably be another bar."

"I don't like any of it," Jonas said.

"Either do I," Wilson said.

At one minute to midnight, Nels woke Novelee up, they counted down to midnight, kissed and clinked their drinks. Then, they walked down to the beach, where the bonfire blazed and watched the fireworks.

Brilliant colors streamed into the sky illuminating the ocean below. People cheered.

A drunken Nels yelled out "two thousand and twelve, two thousand and twelve, two thousand and twelve!"

A few minutes later, Wilson announced he was taking Fabiola back to his apartment for an hour or so.

"I thought you said you didn't feel comfortable with it," Nels said, through the Bohemia fog.

Even in the moonlight, Nels could see Wilson's bloodshot eyes. He was quite drunk. Fabiola had saddled up to him standing by the fire and begun rubbing him seductively, in places reserved for intimacy.

Wilson had a mischievous smile on his face. "Just for a few hours, then we'll meet you at the Gym bar."

"I don't think it's a good idea," Nels said. "I don't trust that chick."

"Just for an hour," Wilson said.

"If you're not back in an hour I'm coming to check on you," Nels said.

Chapter Twenty

1:33 am, Sunday, January 1, 2012, Atlantic One, Room Number Eight, Costambar.

Fabiola was on top and Wilson enjoyed fondling her ample breasts while making love to her. If there was anything that puzzled him, it was her expression-deadpan.

He laughed and smiled as they girated, trying to get her to follow suit. Her expression remained unchanged.

Through some scribbling on a piece of paper, Wilson had managed to negotiate two hours for 1,500 pesos-probably the going rate anyway.

The fact was he hadn't been laid for about six months, which is why ultimately he had given in to Fabiola's advances.

Suddenly the door popped open and Eduardo stormed in, wielding his large knife. He wasn't going to take any chances as he knew the Atlantic One was a secure building and he had to be quick.

Fabiola jumped off in mock surprise and attacked Eduardo, swinging her right fist. It was no match for the knife, however, and he slashed her forearm, deeper and longer than he wanted, but he hoped it would look good for the police. Blood squirted out and she crumpled to the floor, holding her wound.

Wearing a black face mask, Eduardo was on Wilson immediately. First he told him if he screamed he would die and secondly he demanded to know where the money was. Wilson was smart enough to have two stashes and he pointed to the first, under his mattress.

Eduardo tipped part of the mattress up, removed a wad of cash, sliced Wilson from his neck right down to his naval, and exited the room, making sure to grab the laptop on the way out. He winked at Fabiola as he watched the blood squirt from Wilson's gaping wound.

By that time, she had a towel wrapped around her arm.

When the door closed behind him, Wilson screamed.

Nels arrived at the scene a little while later. Novelee and Jonas waited in the Gym Bar. By that time paramedics and police were in the room, questioning Fabiola and readying both of them for transport to Centre Medico Bournigal.

Paramedics had Fabiola's arm bandaged and had stemmed the bleeding.

They were struggling to stem the tide of Wilson's bleeding. He was losing a lot of blood and the white sheets were now mostly red.

"Happy New Year," Wilson said, managing a weak smile. "I should have listened to you."

"Was she a part of it?" Nels asked.

"I don't know. It looked to me like she tried to defend me, and took a large slash for her troubles." Wilson's voice grew weaker as he spoke and he eventually closed his eyes.

"Hang in there buddy," Nels said as he was wheeled out of the room on a stretcher.

Fabiola walked to the ambulance and got in the back with Wilson. The siren blared and it zipped away.

Chapter Twenty-One

2:15 pm, Monday, January 2nd, Nels' apartment, Costambar.

Nels scrolled through his many emails, stopping at one that caught his attention, regarding his father. It was from his niece Kathy, the twenty-four year old daughter of his sister Denise.

It read: Uncle Nels, please give us a call asap, either myself Grandma, or my Mom.

Nels had been told earlier that his father had been admitted to the hospital for colon cancer. The latest update he had read said the surgery had gone reasonably well but staff would be transporting his father Charlie into a chronic care facility.

Nels had translated it to mean his days were numbered and they weren't able to remove all the cancer. His mother Melanie had confirmed this in an earlier Skype conversation. She had said the doctors were giving him one to six months to live.

Nels had hoped he would be able to visit his father after he returned to Calgary.

And when he had been told his father was in hospital, he did have an option to return. But, he had never gotten along with Charlie. In fact, he had been smacked around quite a bit as a young boy. He had surmised long ago that his father was just not a nice man. He hadn't spoken to him in twenty years. And he knew now that he would never speak to him again. At least not in his conscious life.

Nels was also worried about the tragic events of late.

Wilson had been flown back to Calgary due to complications with his injuries. So far, his fate was unknown.

Jonas had returned to Sosewer to continue down the road to perdition.

Novelee had been upset by events and, when it was discovered that a hundred dollars had gone missing from Nels's bedroom, she had decided to leave. She looked out of sorts as she had left.

Nels knew both of them had been in the bedroom changing on New Year's Eve, while they prepared for the party. He thought it was Fabiola who stole the money and he also suspected she was in cahoots with the man who had tried to kill Wilson.

It was all the same to Nels. On New Year's Day he was recovering from a massive headache and hangover-and he wanted the day to sleep, gather his thoughts and clear his head.

Last night he had started a new sleeping pill called Sedoxil and he liked how it worked. It put him out and, unlike Zopiclone, did not make him drowsy the next afternoon. It also seemed to mix well with alcohol.

Nels read the email again and his thoughts returned to Belinda and Simon, arriving tomorrow afternoon. They were in danger. Of that he was certain.

He picked up the phone and dialed his niece. Since he had slept most of the day, his head finally felt like it was somewhat clear. But he had yet to have his first rum and fruit juice. That would come after this call.

The phone rang twice and Kathy picked it up. "Kathy, how are you?" Nels asked.

Of all his nieces, and he had four, Kathy was his favorite. She had already secured a good paying job working in a hospital as a patient care aide. The position had required two years of education and she had completed it with high marks. She had a stable relationship and owned a house with her boyfriend of six years. She had her head screwed on properly. Nels liked that about her.

"I'm okay considering. Are you still in the DR?"

"Yeah."

A long pause. "I don't want to be the one to spoil your vacation but your father died yesterday morning, New Year's Day, at about eight o'clock. It seemed like he was doing well but when they moved him to the chronic care facility, he just didn't make it"

"It's okay Kathy. It's not your fault." A long pause. "Just so you know I am not inclined to go back to Brantford for the funeral."

Kathy knew the history. It required no explanation. "That's okay uncle Nels, if it doesn't work for you. But I would like you to come and visit us sometime."

Nels felt sad he hadn't gotten to know this special person better. He supposed a lot of it was the distance factor. He lived three thousand miles away, and other than a fairly close relationship with his mother, he had grown apart from his other siblings-three brothers and two sisters.

"Sure, I can do that sometime. I would like to get to know you better."

"How's the DR been treating you?"

"Good. Listen Kathy, sweetie, I'm going to call my mom, just to see what she thinks of my plans. I'm going to let you go now. Take care."

Kathy said goodbye and Nels clicked the red phone on Skype, ending the call. He had been tempted to tell her he loved her, but it seemed so long since they had talked. It just didn't feel right. Maybe, sometime in the future they would have a closer relationship that would warrant such terms of endearment.

He got up from his computer on his kitchen table, positioned in the middle of the living room with a view out through the balcony, opened the fridge and mixed himself a strong rum and fruit juice. He walked out to the balcony and took a sip. It was a hot sunny day, clear blue sky and hardly a cloud. A gentle breeze blew. He took another sip of the rum punch, and tried to assess his emotions.

If he had to be completely honest, he would say he felt a little sad-but not sad enough to cry. And why should he change his plans, travel all the way to Brantford for the funeral of a man who was his biological father-but certainly not a father in any other sense of the word?

He took a long pull on the drink, returned to Skype and called his mom. They had been divorced for over twenty-five years-and to say they were good friends was a stretch.

After some perfunctory conversation, his mother said, "Well if it's going to interrupt your plans too much in the DR, you should just stay there."

After that she quickly changed the subject, not even wanting to dwell on the death any longer. She asked him questions about the DR, his girlfriend and the local culture.

After a short conversation, he hung up feeling satisfied. He gulped the drink, finishing it off.

Tomorrow I'm going on the offensive, he thought.

Chapter Twenty-Two

8:56 pm, Monday, January 2nd, black apartment building on a hill, Puerto Plata.

Nels sat outside the building waiting. He was in a rented green 1992 Honda Prelude. He watched the foot traffic coming and going from the apartment.

He knew Belinda and Simon were inside having dinner and drinks, waiting for his arrival.

But he waited for the arrival of someone else-Eduardo.

Since he had spotted the man a few weeks back-his gut told him he was responsible for slashing Wilson.

And he knew with an eerie certainty that Eduardo planned to rob and kill Belinda and Simon.

He glanced at the hand cannon on the passenger seat next to him, picked it up and checked to make sure the safety was off. It was.

Suddenly he asked himself, "What the fuck am I doing here?"

"Oh, right," he answered. "Trying to prevent the death of my good friends."

He remembered going to the police and getting nowhere. He also remembered talking to Juan, the owner and bodyguard in his apartment complex. He had been sympathetic to Nels' concerns but was unwilling to help. But he had provided Nels with an untraceable handgun.

Nels was going to take the law into his own hands.

He picked the gun up again, felt its weight. He was convinced it would do the job. He tucked it into his jeans and resumed his surveillance. He couldn't remember where he had rented the car but that didn't surprise him.

Since his days in the DR, there were some things he just couldn't remember anymore. He chalked it up to the Bohemia fog. Or maybe his mind was just too full-and he would have to forget a few things to make room to remember more.

He noticed a motoconcho pull up to the building and stop. A small man got off the bike and handed the driver something-probably a hundred peso note.

Was it him? Nels picked up his binoculars and adjusted the focus. He was parked directly across the street from the building. He could barely make out the man's features because of the darkness.

But the streetlamp illuminated the man just enough. Nels squinted.

No. That man was much too old and fat to be Eduardo. He put his binoculars down as the man entered the building and the motoconcho sped away.

Where did I get these binoculars? He didn't have an answer.

A few minutes later, a taxi screeched to a halt in front of the building. A small man, fitting the description of Eduardo, jumped out and sprinted to the apartment entrance. The taxi squealed its tires and sped away.

There was something in the man's hand. Was it a gun?

Nels wasn't about to take any chances. He jerked at the driver door handle.

Shit. It wouldn't open. *How do I unlock this fucking thing?* He fiddled with the knobs. Nothing seemed to work. Finally he turned the interior light on, located the door lock, quickly unlocked it and jumped out. As he landed, he tripped on the curb, falling hard on the concrete. A dog barked, punctuating his grunt as he slowly got up and checked for the revolver. It was there.

He was about to sprint across the street when it suddenly became busy with automobile and motoconcho traffic.

Horns blared, two stroke motors rattled and cars hissed by. The noise was deafening.

Although it was only a few minutes, it seemed like hours had gone by before Nels noticed a small window of opportunity.

He reacted quickly and leaped off the curb. A motoconcho honked its horn twice as it narrowly missed him. He was in the middle of the road when a large truck appeared out of nowhere- its air horn booming out an earsplitting warning.

Nels increased his strides and hurdled toward the curb, arching his back like an Olympic athlete to maximize the distance of his long-jump.

The truck missed him by inches as he hit the curb, immediately somersaulting to avoid injury. He leaped up from the rolling somersault, continuing his sprint. He was thankful he had practiced that move many times as a teenager, jumping off garage roofs for entertainment.

He ran up the stairs, reached the top floor and raced down the hall to Belinda and Simon's apartment. The door was closed and he heard muffled screams coming from the room.

He winced as he noticed the number four on the apartment door, steadying himself to kick it in. With one kick the door flew open, smashing into the inside wall with such force it dislodged the top hinges.

Nels eyes widened, seeing the macabre scene in front of him.

Belinda was tied to a sofa in the living room, buck naked with her arms and legs outstretched. Her mouth was contorted with fear and her eyes bulged in their sockets. She had multiple stab wounds that oozed blood, and a clean incision-like slit across her throat- probably the final death cut after Eduardo had had his way with her.

Simon was tied to a chair, blood dripping from ropes tied to his ankles and wrists. He was gagged with a white cloth and when he saw Nels enter, a muffled sound came from his gag.

The words were incomprehensible but the tone was unmistakable-he wanted help.

Eduardo stood over Simon with a machete to his throat and smiled.

Nels instinctively fired the gun at Eduardo and the bullet whizzed by his head, missing by inches, and chewing into the wooden window frame behind.

Eduardo smiled again, cut Simon's throat with the machete, turned, raced out to the balcony and leaped off, disappearing into the night.

"No, no, no," Nels said, running to his friend and putting his hands to his throat, trying to stem the flow of blood. It was no use. He watched the life drain out of him as blood squirted between his fingers.

He heard a loud banging at the door. Wait a minute. There was no door. A voice accompanied the knocks. "Nels, Nels, Nels!"

He jerked upright in bed, was just about to scream, and suddenly realized where he was-in his apartment bedroom.

The knock again. "Nels, are you okay?"

He recognized the voice. It was his friend Juan.

"One minute," Nels said getting up and walking into the bathroom. He turned on the tap, splashed some cold water in his face, and wiped it dry with a towel.

He opened the door in his underwear. Juan looked at him, puzzled, and apologized. "I'm sorry to disturb you. Are you okay?"

"Yeah. A nightmare."

"Sorry to hear it."

"Is your girlfriend here?"

"No."

"I heard you screaming and I thought something was wrong. So I came down to check on you."

Nels was happy he had a friend like Juan, who lived right above him, possessed an arsenal of weapons and had told him on more than one occasion he would defend him with his life. He had the classic good looks of Antonio Banderas, with a slightly darker skin tone.

"I'm glad you did. Thanks."

"I was looking for you on New Year's Eve. Wanted to party with you."

Nels thought if Juan and Oria had been along maybe Wilson would not now be sitting in an intensive care unit in a Calgary hospital.

"I was at El Farolito," Nels said.

"Did you have a good time?"

"We'll talk about that soon."

"Okay. Do you want to go out to Bananas with us tonight?"

"What time is it?" Nels asked.

"Ten thirty," Juan said, looking at his cell phone.

"Okay, give me a half hour to clean up and I'll meet you poolside."

"Good," Juan said, smiling. Nels staggered into the bathroom, finally remembering he had gone down for a nap after a few rum punches.

One of the things he liked about Juan-he was always smiling.

He could well turn out to be Nels' best-and only-Dominican friend. And Nels knew he needed him now more than ever.

Chapter Twenty-Three

10:56 pm, Monday, January 2nd, Banana Bar, Costambar

"Are you telling me three thousand pesos is all a life is worth around here?" Nels asked Juan for the second time. *That's only about eighty dollars!*

They sat in the popular bar and restaurant. Bachata music thumped out, people danced, laughed and chatted amicably. It was a typical Dominican bar. Although ex-pats also loved it, on this night the mix was about sixty-forty in favor of the Dominicans. Nels drank Bohemia and Juan sipped whiskey. Oria, his pleasingly plump girlfriend, was a Cuba libre woman.

Nels had filled Juan in on his nightmares, the near death of his friend Wilson, and had provided descriptions of Eduardo and Fabiola along with his hunches regarding them. He had told Juan that not only did he fear for his own life, but especially for the lives of his friends Belinda and Simon, who would be arriving tomorrow afternoon.

He had also learned Fabiola had stolen some clothes from Novelee during that ill-fated New Year's Eve party. She had informed him during an earlier phone conversation that she was on the hunt for her. She assured Nels if she found her she would beat the shit out of her to get her clothes back.

Nels knew Novelee wasn't above violence, particularly when it meant retrieving what little clothes she now owned.

Nels had only protested briefly, knowing full well that in the ghetto where Novelee lived there was a pecking order. Novelee had a reputation and many of the women feared her.

She could not take the theft of her clothes from a much younger woman lying down. Even if it meant risking her life to try and get them back.

Nels conveniently left Novelee out of the conversation, not wanting to leave Juan with the impression he hung around with such a wild tempered and potentially uncontrollable woman.

Juan looked around the bar, adjusted the piece tucked into his jeans. "Please keep your voice down," he said to Nels.

"Sorry," Nels said, glancing around nervously.

Juan slid his chair closer to Nels. "Javier will kill anyone I ask him to for three thousand pesos. He is a corrupt cop in Costambar, in fact a high level cop. There will be no investigation, I promise you that."

"And you don't want to get involved personally?" Nels asked.

"I would," Juan said without hesitation. "But if Eduardo and Fabiola die at my hands it may lead to you and by default to me. I live one floor above you. The police already know Wilson is a friend of yours. You have motive."

A few ex-pats whom Nels knew glanced at him as he talked. He looked at them and smiled. *They probably wonder why all of a sudden I need a two hundred and fifty pound muscle bound bodyguard.*

"Okay, so what do I need to do to get this underway," Nels asked.

"Give me the three thousand pesos and I will give the instructions to Javier. Six thousand if you want them both dead."

"Does he know Fabiola?"

"Yes. And he knows where she lives. She will lead him to Eduardo, who has been elusive for some time."

"Did you know Eduardo is currently wanted on a number of other murders? He was positively identified in at least three of them."

"I didn't know. But it doesn't surprise me," Nels said.

"Okay, let's do this," Nels said. "One more thing."

"What's that?" Juan asked.

"I'd feel much safer if you picked up my friends at the airport tomorrow. I have a taxi driver who packs a gun and is also ex-military. But he's a much smaller man than you. I'd feel more comfortable if you were there. I'll pay you if you want."

"I'll do it and you don't have to pay me," Juan said, smiling. "No problem brother." He put his big arm around Nels' shoulder. "Everything will be taken care of. Now, let's have another drink, shall we, and talk of more positive things. How are things with your girlfriend?"

Chapter Twenty-Four

10:56 am, Tuesday, January 3rd, Centro Medico Bournigal, Puerto Plata.

"I have some good news for you," the doctor told Novelee after bringing in the throat x-ray recently paid for by Nels. "Nothing shows up on the x-ray."

Novelee breathed a sigh of relief.

"And you say the new pills are working much better?"

"Yes," Novelee said. "It took a few days but I don't have much throat pain right now."

"That's good. Now let's see if this new vitamin regiment will help bring your energy level back. How is your appetite?"

"Getting better," Novelee said.

"Headaches, stomach aches, mood swings?"

"No headache, stomach ache, but I do notice sometimes my moods still shift quickly."

"That should improve the longer you're on this new prescription," the doctor said.

"Now, let's see you again January 20th, at two."

Novelee left the hospital feeling elated and sad. Elated because she thought she was dying and now her health had taken a turn for the better. And there was nothing in her throat that would require an operation.

Sad, because, she had found out today her parents were renting out their house in Puerto Plata and moving to the country. Her brother had built a small house for them on his acreage and it seemed wise for them to move into it. He had offered to let them live there for free and they could grow vegetables and live off the rental income from their three-bedroom apartment, which they owned clear title.

Since Novelee's father had been laid off, the family had suffered long stretches without food. At least this plan would allow them to eat. The other family members who would occasionally pop by for a free meal-well now they would be on their own.

The family simply did not have the means to look after them anymore. The five thousand pesos per month they had managed to rent their apartment for would be barely enough to feed themselves. They would have to be extremely resourceful and frugal to survive on that.

Novelee stood outside the house she had grown up in teary eyed as the last of the family's belongings were packed into a waiting truck.

She hugged and kissed her mother and father and off they went. Her and Papito stood curbside, crying and waving as the vehicle pulled away.

She felt alone and empty. She still slept on the tile floor of her cousin's apartment on top of a thin comforter. It was anything but soft and she had no privacy. Not to mention no job and hardly any clothes.

Which reminded her of Fabiola. So she wiped her tears away, took her son into her cousin's apartment, and left in pursuit of the woman who had stolen her clothes.

She knew exactly where Fabiola lived. And she was in the mood to kick some ass.

But it only took her fifteen minutes to learn that Fabiola had moved to Santiago-maybe permanently, her friends had said.

She's scared shitless of me that's why she left, Novelee thought, as she opened her cell phone to call Nels.

Chapter Twenty-Five

2:30 pm, Tuesday, January 3rd, en route to the airport, Puerto Plata.

"I haven't seen these sugar cane fields cut down in over four and half years," Juan explained as they drove along the highway.

Nels looked at his phone. He had just received another text message from Novelee, saying she missed him. She had called him earlier in the day, informing him that Fabiola was now living in Santiago, about an hour away from Puerto Plata. She also mentioned the good news about her health and said she would like to get together soon to get drunk and make love all day. She wanted to celebrate.

In spite of the stress he was feeling, the call had stirred up some sexual desire. But he had told her he was picking up some friends at the airport this afternoon and would probably be busy with them until late in the evening.

He had promised to call her in the morning. He looked up from his phone, noticing Juan watching him from the corner of his eye.

"Why haven't the fields been cut?" he asked.

"The sugar cane factory around here went under."

"Why?"

"Apparently they owed over $60 million US to some American creditors and they couldn't pay it back. The government refused to get involved so they went belly up."

"Unfortunate, given all the sugar cane around here," Nels said.

"Look around," Juan said. "All these fields used to be sugar cane, and Montellano is a sugar cane town."

"I know the real estate in the DR has taken a real nosedive since the recession," Nels said.

"Huge," Juan agreed. "Tourism numbers, despite what you read, are way down. Four of the five star hotels in Playa Dorada closed recently."

"I heard," Nels said.

"A number of airlines have also cut the flights to Puerto Plata," Juan said. "They want the tourists to go to Punta Cana, where all the money on infrastructure and hotels has just been spent."

"A few years ago, local banks would pay eight to ten percent interest on the equivalent of a savings account. Now you would be lucky to get four percent. That puts a lot of pressure on the lower, and middle classes. And the poor. They can barely feed themselves from day to day."

"I've seen some examples," Nels said.

"Which is why it has created such a spike in the crime rate. I don't know what the stats will tell you but I'll tell you as a Dominican there are more Dominicans preying on foreigners for their money than ever before."

"I can just feel the negative vibe in the air," Nels said.

"And I'll tell you something else," Juan said. "It makes me embarrassed to be Dominican to know what kind of vultures we have here. I'm embarrassed about that part of my culture."

"Not your fault," Nels said. "Besides, there are a lot of good Dominicans, like you."

"Yeah but there are many more bad ones now, because of the economy," Juan said. "Do you know the police in Puerto

Plata have started killing thieves in the streets, even very young kids."

"I didn't know," Nels said.

"Well, a lot of this stuff will not find its way into the papers, but thieves are getting killed here. The police want to send a message to them, because our economy is so dependent on tourism, and the numbers are so low."

You learn so much more about the culture when you have a Dominican friend, Nels thought.

"And be very careful with the women you hang around with. You might trust your girlfriend, but never, never trust any of her friends. And don't let them into your apartment."

Nels thought of the trouble he had gotten Wilson into by hooking him up. And he had also noticed a few days ago, in addition to the money that was missing from his apartment, that his netbook had been stolen. On a whim, he had decided to open the computer bag, where he had last put it and noticed it missing. He used two computers-a small laptop and a netbook, which he had packed away into his computer bag a few weeks back-knowing that he couldn't hook it up anyway as his computer connection was hard-wired.

Without a splitter cable, which he couldn't be bothered to purchase, he could only hook up one computer at a time. And he preferred the laptop to the netbook as the monitor and keyboard were much bigger and more conducive to longer stretches of work.

Yesterday he had noticed the netbook had vanished. After going through the list of suspects-it was obviously an inside job-one person stood out-Fabiola. When she had entered the apartment with Novelee on New Year's Eve, Nels and his friends had remained poolside drinking beer.

She had probably slipped it into her purse and it had long been sold.

Nels decided not to tell Juan about the netbook theft. He felt so stupid for letting his guard down and he knew the mention of it would lead to Novelee and would mean her reputation in Costambar would be instantly trashed-she would never be able to acquire work in the community-in fact she would probably be barred from it.

As much as he had issues with Novelee, he also had a three-year history with her. He had never noticed anything missing in the past-not even as much as a hundred pesos. He also noticed her reaction when he had mentioned it to her-one of surprise and not guilt. Unless she was an expert, he couldn't detect any tells in her eyes.

Although the netbook was only worth a couple of hundred dollars and had nothing valuable on it, Nels was pissed off at himself for letting his guard down. When he had discovered it missing, he had spent the whole day fuming-even though he knew intellectually it was no way to deal with it.

They arrived at the airport and Juan pressed the button for the parking ticket-a mere 35 pesos.

Belinda and Simon stood curbside waving-they had timed it perfectly.

Chapter Twenty-Six

3:30 pm, Wednesday, January 4th, poolside, Nels' apartment, Costambar.

They sat in the same green chairs underneath the same green umbrella drinking beer. Nels, Jonas, Novelee and another friend that Jonas had brought along. Her name was Irene.

Jonas had decided to check out of the Sewer for a few days and spend some time with Nels and his new friend. He had checked into the well maintained complex on the main drag of Costambar called Villas Lirio. Who knew how long he would hang around.

Nels had explained to Jonas that if Irene went up to the apartment to go to the bathroom, he had to accompany her. He wanted her watched like a hawk.

There was something about her right off the bat that Nels didn't like. She was a dark skinned diminutive thing with small features and a tight little body. By her admission she was twenty- eight years old.

Her small dark eyes were attractive but shifty. Jonas had met her in a Sosua disco and had decided to bring her to Costambar for a few nights. Apparently, she was an energetic dynamo in bed.

But there was something about her demeanor that bothered Nels-and he couldn't put a finger on it.

Maybe he was just put off by the fact that Belinda and Simon had not heeded his warning, and he still worried about them. It didn't help that they checked into an apartment in Puerto Plata, albeit an upscale neighborhood.

But the number on their door was four.

Maybe it was the fact for the last few nights he hadn't slept well and was being haunted by his nightmares.

Maybe it was Novelee's mood swings and his increasing unease about her.

Maybe he just felt like it was time to get the hell out of here while the getting was good.

He didn't know exactly why but his patience was wearing thin. Of course, the Bohemia and Brutal fog didn't help matters.

Irene had her hands and legs all over Jonas as they drank their beer. Jonas, to his credit, finally gently pushed her off and shifted his chair away-telling her there was plenty of time for that later.

Nels asked her some questions. Some of the answers just didn't add up. She said she ran a manicure and pedicure business from her home. When Nels asked her about the business hours her reply was "I work whenever I want."

Which meant that she would never get any loyal clientele if they never knew when her business was open. Stupid answer.

Her asked her if she had to work tomorrow. "If I feel like it," she replied.

Novelee, becoming tired of the interrogation, jumped in. Her mood had become questionable. "Don't get so fresh with her," she said to Nels. "Or I'll give you a smack."

Nels was not in the mood for any shit related to violence. "Listen, you can talk to anyone else in your family or friends like that, but not to me. You talk to me like that you know where the door is."

There was a long pause.

Finally, Novelee said "Okay, but I was only joking."

The mood lightened up again.

The women began talking in Spanish while Nels and Jonas conversed in English.

"I heard this one story," Jonas began. "A Canadian guy meets this Dominican woman, goes out on a few dates, and then suddenly she starts asking him for money. No surprise, but this time he won't give it to her. She demands two thousand pesos and he tells her to take a hike."

"Well, she leaves, punches herself in the face so hard she gives herself two black eyes. The police here do not take kindly to women beaters. So, a few days later the cops show up with a court summons charging him with assault. He ends up going to court, and to avoid a trial, has to pay the woman five thousand pesos."

"That should surprise me but it doesn't," Nels said, taking a long pull on his beer. "I met this girl on the beach here a few years back, before I met Novelee. Well, one thing led to another and next thing I know she's up in my apartment. A few drinks later and were in the sack. Well, we finish up and she starts asking me right away if she can move in with me. She said she'd look after the apartment when I returned to Canada and be there for me when I arrive back. As long as I paid for everything."

"She probably has about five foreigners paying for her now," Jonas said.

"Probably," Nels agreed.

"Hey, I got this business idea," Jonas suddenly said, smiling mischievously.

"Oh what's that?" Nels asked.

"You know the public bathrooms they have in Sosua, the ones for ten pesos?"

"Yeah."

"Well, we should build our own, right down the beach from the other one."

Nels knew he wasn't serious. "That would piss off the other guy. He takes pride in his work, sitting outside the bathrooms all day, collecting his pesos."

"I know exactly how we can promote it," Jonas said.

"How? Nels asked, suddenly laughing at the whole nutty concept.

"I can attend to the patrons and you can walk the beach promoting our new bano. I'll make up coupons that you can distribute on the beach, offering two bathroom visits for the price of one. We can even tell them we've got the softest ass wipe in the country."

"I think we can make a go of it," Nels said.

"Let's drink to our new partnership," Jonas said, laughing.

A few hours later, they went to Pasqual's on the beach and had some food and drinks. Soon it was nearing six thirty in the evening. So they went their separate ways and agreed to hook up later.

Nels took Novelee back to his apartment for a love making session. They were both a little hot and bothered and it was thoroughly enjoyable. Sometimes, her negativity faded, and her eyes took on a deeply passionate look, making her absolutely stunning and irresistible.

It didn't hurt that-although a little on the skinny side-her body was beautiful.

It was a few minutes after the session that things turned ugly.

"You certainly could have picked a better apartment," she said, as they sat on the balcony sipping Cuba libres, watching the stars and listening to the crickets. "Everything in this place is shit. The bathroom needs work, the kitchen needs work, some windows are missing screens and it's a mosquito haven. Even that other place you were living in was much better."

"I don't think so," Nels said. "That place started to self-destruct." He wondered how a woman living with a middle-aged couple with a two year old baby girl, sleeping on the tile floor of their tiny one room apartment with her son could possibly complain about the likes of his large apartment. At least she had a soft bed, privacy, food, drink and a TV with Nels.

And he gave her money almost daily.

He was about to kick her out when Jonas and Irene arrived. He decided to take a cup of shut the fuck up and see if the whole thing would blow over. A few minutes later, it did and they were laughing and talking again.

But, he had to admit her comments had left him with a bad taste in his mouth-and had soured his otherwise cheerful mood.

Chapter Twenty-Seven

3:30 pm, Thursday, January 5th, Puerto Plata.

Nels honked the horn-one long beep- as the little boy scurried across the street, narrowly avoiding getting struck by a car.

A motoconcho honked behind him-two short beeps-which meant he was about to pass. A split second later, he passed Nels.

The horns in the DR actually meant something. It was a complicated language that you had to understand to navigate the roads successfully. Nels knew two short beeps generally meant they were going to pass you, or they were entering an intersection, and wanted everyone to know that-subject to last minute change-they were coming through.

Two long beeps, now that was another story. It generally meant, "Get the hell out of the way, I'm coming through."

Maybe it was part of the Dominican machismo, but they seemed to enjoy playing chicken on the roads.

The other trick to driving is not to hesitate. He who hesitates is lost. Even worse is to hesitate and then go, which is asking for trouble.

But Nels understood the Dominicans didn't mean any offense by all the horn honking-they just want motion. And, usually the drivers with the biggest balls of steel got to their destinations much quicker.

Of course, the North American view of horn honking often results in anger, frequent use of the index finger-and worst case scenario-road rage and death.

Death was what was on Nels' mind as he cautiously navigated the vehicle-a tan Chevy Trailblazer- through the busy streets.

He was on his way to pick up his friends, Belinda and Simon, and they had plans to go to Costambar for dinner and a few drinks.

He had rented the vehicle from Juan-just for the day-so he could drive his friends around Puerto Plata for some sightseeing-maybe see the popular but noisy beachside Malecon first, go for dinner in Costambar, and visit the casino at nearby Ocean World later in the evening.

But what bothered him was that he was driving a vehicle in Puerto Plata to pick up his friends. While there were obviously a few things different, it seemed eerily like his nightmare he had in Calgary before leaving. Not to mention his more recent and much more tragic nightmare.

Jonas and Irene had left his apartment at about 11:00 pm last night, sensing that Nels was a little out of sorts. After they left, Novelee started telling him about her Facebook page, saying she had pictures of herself showing lots of cleavage and was receiving a lot of friend requests.

Nels didn't know if this tact was designed to make him jealous and therefore more in love with her, but he didn't want any part of it-and wasn't interested in looking up her Facebook page.

Instead he had taken a Sedoxil and gone to bed shortly afterward, leaving Novelee to sleep on the mattress he had dragged out into the living room and placed in front of the television. She loved watching TV, particularly the soap opera, Esmerelda. It was full of drama.

In the morning she had received a call from a woman who owned a manicure salon. Novelee had helped her in the past and the woman said one of her employees had gone to Santo Domingo on a family emergency, and she needed a replacement for a few days.

"I've got a job," Novelee had announced smiling, before calling her motoconcho taxi and leaving.

After her comments the previous night, Nels had been happy to get rid of her for a few days-give him some time to make sure his friends were out of danger. Over the past few days, he had learned a few things about Miss Innocent that had surprised him.

Apparently, she had a bit of a history with foreigners and in a drunken moment had told him she had had a number of foreign boyfriends, and had even been married to a German and lived in Costambar for three years. Her German ex had provided her plenty of money monthly, and according to Novelee the reason they divorced was that he had kept her indoors on many occasions against her will. She had equated the experience to being in prison.

She certainly knew what that was like.

Nels checked his map-he didn't have the benefit of a GPS-and pulled onto a street he believed Belinda and Simon were staying.

He finally recognized the building and pulled alongside the curb, finding a parking spot right in front of the unit.

It was sunny and hot. A gentle breeze blew in from the ocean. The well-maintained complex was gated, and he had to call Belinda from his cell, while standing outside.

A few minutes later, they were in the SUV and off to the Malecon, the public beach that fronted a main thoroughfare in Puerto Plata. Belinda sat in the front seat next to Nels and Simon sat in the back.

Nels had briefed Belinda and Simon on the attack on their friend Wilson, and they were all a little nervous as they drove along the Malecon, watching the ocean, the little restaurants and bars, the tourists and Dominicans walking on the beach, swimming in the ocean and talking amicably.

Looked like everyone was having a good time, although Nels had heard a tourist had been recently held up at gunpoint and robbed in broad daylight on the Malecon.

"Would you like to stop for a drink?" Belinda asked, after some small talk. She managed a smile, in spite of the black cloud that hung over them. Belinda was full of energy and determined to put the bad news out of her mind, so they could enjoy their vacation.

Nels hadn't bothered to tell them he had hired a hit-man to take out Fabiola and Eduardo. *Too much information*, he thought, as he acknowledged Belinda's request with a nod, found a parking spot and pulled in.

A few minutes later, they sat enjoying their drinks, looking out at the beach and watching the pedestrian foot traffic. Other than the high-pitched rumble of the two stroke motoconchos screaming by, the area was quite pleasant.

Recently, the municipal government had undertaken to completely redo the public walkway, lining the beach, as well as many of the stairwell entry ways down onto the sand. Nels thought the infrastructure was flawed by design. Why put a six lane thorough-fare right next to an otherwise nice beach? It didn't make a lot of sense to him. But, then again, neither did a lot of other things here.

"Have you heard anything about Wilson?" Belinda asked, sipping her Cuba libre. She had decided to take a break from her gin and tonic and sample the Anejo, dark local rum.

Simon was otherwise engaged in watching the attractive Dominican women stroll the Malecon. A few of them smiled at him as they passed. He sipped his Bohemia beer and smiled back.

Nels reached for his drink, scanning the foot traffic nervously. He also had a Cuba libre, but the rum he drank was Columbus, which he found a little smoother to his palate. He knew if he got too drunk to walk, he could always take the car.

He wasn't worried about an impaired driving charge in the DR. Money could almost always get you out of any vehicular incident that involved the police. He finished his drink and held up three fingers to the waitress.

She came over and put three drinks down on the table and smiled as she followed Nels' eyes. She had long black hair, her skin was dark enough to indicate she was probably Haitian born. Her breasts stood out as one of her best features, protruding from her tight white, V-neck shirt. To say she displayed ample cleavage was an understatement.

"Earth to Nels," Belinda said.

"Oh, sorry, I did get a call from him this morning."

"And?"

"Apparently the large gash didn't penetrate any major organs, although it sliced through part of his stomach lining."

"Will he recover okay?" she asked, momentarily shifting her eyes to Simon, who noticed the slightly annoyed glance and removed his eyes from two attractive and sexily dressed Dominican women walking by.

"Is he going to be okay?" Simon asked, suddenly concerned.

"I think so," Nathan said. "At least that's what I'm told."

"I sure hope so," Belinda said, concern etching her brow. Both Simon and Belinda were also friends of Wilson. Nels didn't have a lot of friends, but there was some overlap with the dozen or so he did have.

"Me too," Nels agreed returning his gaze to a beat up tan Toyota Tercel that had squealed to a stop about fifty feet behind his parked Trailblazer.

He noticed the driver in the car and his heart suddenly skipped a beat. If it wasn't Eduardo, it was a body double.

"Time to go," he said, slapping seven hundred pesos on the bar, more than enough to cover the drinks. Belinda was taking a sip of her drink, as he grabbed her arm, pulling her out of her chair. The glass fell out of her hand and shattered on the concrete, the brown liquid spilling out.

Heads turned at the restaurant as they ran to the vehicle. Nels hit the remote opener. Belinda and Simon jumped in the backseat on the passenger side as Nels ran around to the driver door. As he opened it, he glanced behind him and saw Eduardo approaching, gun drawn and pointed at his head.

He ducked as a bullet whizzed by his head, hopped in the vehicle and started it quickly.

"Duck," he said to Belinda and Simon. Belinda was screaming, but she stopped long enough to follow his instructions, just as two bullets shattered the rear-view window and ripped through the upholstery, narrowly missing them.

Eduardo walked methodically toward them firing, oblivious to frantic stares and screams that echoed from passersby.

Nels slammed the vehicle into drive, didn't bother shoulder checking and floored it out of his parking spot, tires squealing. A motoconcho crashed into the side of the SUV, sending the driver flying over it and tumbling onto the road. Two more bullets chewed into the back metal door as he made his escape.

Eduardo ran back to his vehicle, jumped in and began his pursuit.

"You guys okay?" Nels asked, as he sped down the Malecon, honking his horn and weaving in and out of traffic. He had it floored.

Belinda had stopped screaming. "Yeah," she said.

Simon popped his head up and nodded.

Nels checked the rearview mirror. Eduardo was right on their ass. *Fuck!*

He handed his phone to Simon as he swerved down a side street, cutting off a couple of motoconchos and another car in the process. They honked their horns in displeasure.

Nels checked the rearview and noticed Eduardo was behind them, although his erratic driving had given them a block or so of distance.

"Look up the contact Juan in there, dial the number and give the phone to me," he said. Simon and Belinda knew not a word of Spanish and Juan knew not a word of English.

It would have to be Nels who would speak to Juan.

It was an old and simple phone and didn't take Simon long to find the number. "Here," he said to Nels after punching in the speed-dial feature. "It's ringing."

He weaved through traffic honking his horn with his left hand, holding the phone to his right ear with the other. Juan picked up after three rings.

"How are you brother?" he asked, recognizing the phone number.

"Not good," Simon said, his voice verging on panic. "I just got shot at five times by Eduardo. He's chasing me now in a tan Toyota Tercel. Where the hell is Javier?"

"Drive toward Costambar, then stay on the highway toward Santiago," Juan said calmly. "I'll call Javier. If he doesn't intercept you I will."

"I'll call you as soon as I pass the Costambar turn-off. It should be less than eight minutes." Nels said, clicking the phone closed, handing it to Simon and jerking the steering wheel hard right, down a narrow pot-holed side street.

The speed was a little too fast and the passenger side wheels left the road briefly. Nels suddenly realized he was driving on two wheels, kept the steering wheel straight and slowed down, allowing the airborne wheels to slam back onto the road, bouncing the SUV completely airborne for a split second before all tires bit the pavement and the vehicle continued on.

"Where the fuck am I going?" he asked, making a mental note the next time he travelled to make a point of getting to know his surroundings a little better before venturing out in a vehicle. He glanced back at his passengers. Belinda's face was white and she was shaking. Her lips had turned purple.

Simon looked concerned but calm. He put a hand on his wife's leg.

Lucky Simon was a map guy. He had not only risen early almost every morning since his arrival to walk for as much as seven miles before returning to the apartment, he had also purchased a Puerto Plata city map and had been studying it for the last few days. Good thing he had a good memory and an even better built in GPS.

"Take a left up there, another right, and that will lead you to the main highway out of Puerto Plata. Turn right on the main highway to get to the Costambar turn-off" he said.

"Thanks," Nels said, looking in the rear-view mirror again. Eduardo had made up some distance. He was now only three or four car lengths behind.

"Hang on," he yelled, slamming on the brakes to avoid a motoconcho that had sped directly into his path. The SUV skidded sideways and Nels released the brakes and accelerated as the shocked driver, who held a half full bottle of rum in his left hand, passed him with inches to spare. He had a little baby sitting in front of him on the bike, another small girl behind him and a fat woman perched sideways on what space remained of the back seat.

"Only four," Nels announced, as he navigated the left turn. "I've seen more than that, and with groceries to boot."

His mind had shifted into self-preservation, adrenaline mode and he was hardly aware of what he had just said.

As he turned, he saw Eduardo with his hand out the window, leveling the gun at them. "Duck again," he said as the shot rang out, this time whizzing past the vehicle and slicing through the wooden door of a ramshackle house on the corner.

Nels wondered if anyone was behind the door as he accelerated and then slowed to prepare for the next sharp right. He heard the sound of gunfire again. "Stay down," he told his friends and ducked his own head trying to point the steering wheel toward where he thought the road was.

The bullet whizzed by. It didn't hit the vehicle. Who knew where it had found a home.

Nels raised his head in time to see the SUV jump the curb, plow into three large blue plastic garbage cans. He righted his course, steered back onto the road as a debris shower hit the windshield. Some white liquid, plastic and paper stuck to the windshield, momentarily blocking his vision.

He hit the wipers and spray simultaneously, rolled down the window, reached over and pulled a few chunks of debris from his line of sight. The wipers smeared the white liquid onto the windshield.

For a moment, the windshield got worse. But, finally the windshield washer fluid and wipers combined, cleared away a tiny area, about eight inches long and four inches high-just enough that when he pressed his head to the glass, he could see where he was going.

"At the top of the hill, that's the highway, turn right," Simon said.

Instead of stopping as he approached the intersection, he accelerated and leaned on the horn-long intermittent beeps-trying to put more distance between him and the killer.

Lots of horns blasted, but by some strange miracle, no vehicles broadsided the SUV as it careened out and merged with the traffic. A few drivers, however, screeched to rather abrupt stops.

As he sped down the highway, Nels glanced in the rearview and breathed a sigh of relief. He had just put a little more distance between him and the killer.

As he approached the Costambar turn-off, he told Simon to dial Juan again. He did so and handed Nels the phone.

"We're approaching the turn-off," Nels said noticing how incredibly calm his voice had become. Even Belinda had stopped shaking.

"Is he behind you?" Juan asked.

"About two blocks, but he's there alright."

"Javier's waiting. He's driving a silver Ford Explorer. He'll be behind Eduardo shortly. Take the fourth left turn, after you pass Costambar."

Nels was getting the picture. "Okay," he said, clicking the phone closed and handing it again to Simon in the back seat. "Count the left turns when we pass the turn-off," he said to Simon. "Tell me when we get to the fourth one."

"Okay," Simon said, looking intently out the window as they raced past a sign that said Costambar with an arrow pointing right. "I'm going to count them out loud."

Nels nodded.

A few seconds later. "One."

Nels checked the rear-view again and now saw the killer and the silver Ford Explorer right behind him. They were leading Eduardo into a trap.

"That's two," Simon said, as Nels stuck his hand on the windshield and removed a few more pieces of the sticky debris. His field of vision had now improved to about a one foot diameter visual opening. Thank God for functioning windshield wipers and washer fluid.

"Three."

Nels noticed the killer had passed a few cars and was now closing the gap. "What the fuck's he got under the hood of that piece of shit," he said.

"Four, right up there, just beyond that bend."

Nels slowed down only slightly to navigate the curve in the road that was just before the fourth turn. A cop passed him going the other way without even a flicker of acknowledgement.

That's fine, Nels thought. *We don't need the police for this one, now do we?*

He skidded onto the dirt road, blowing up a thick cloud of dust as the tires spit out chunks of gravel. The SUV weaved slightly before the tires grabbed and Nels straightened his trajectory and floored it.

The killer was right behind him.

And Javier was right behind the killer, except he wasn't driving. A teenage boy, his protégé Carlos was at the wheel. Javier wasn't about to get distracted by driving. He wanted a clean shot. Maybe two clean shots.

"Speed up a bit Carlos," Javier said to his boy. "But do it slowly."

Carlos smiled and slowly accelerated.

Nels noticed the silver SUV gaining on the killer, so he slowed his speed slightly, hoping to accommodate the hit.

By the time Eduardo noticed the silver SUV coming up behind him it was too late. Javier had straddled himself outside the open passenger window, steadied his arm, and pulled the trigger on his revolver twice. The first bullet shattered the back windshield, penetrating the back of Eduardo's head and head and blowing his brain matter all over the windshield and console.

For good measure, Javier quickly fired a second bullet, which also sliced through Eduardo's skull, about two inches from the first fatal gunshot. More brain matter splattered against the windshield.

Eduardo's head fell forward into the steering wheel, connecting with the horn, causing it to beep loudly and constantly. The vehicle swerved into the ditch, flipped over and came to a crunching stop upside down.

Nels heard the gunshots, saw the vehicle hit the ditch and pulled over, about a hundred feet ahead.

He opened the door, exited the vehicle and watched.

He saw Carlos bring the Explorer to a skidding stop, jump out of the vehicle, douse the overturned Tercel with gasoline and set it ablaze.

Javier never left the vehicle and Nels couldn't see him through the tinted glass.

Carlos smiled and waved at Nels before hopping into the Explorer, fishtailing a U-turn and speeding away from the scene of the crime.

Nels U-turned the Trailblazer and followed suit. Just as he passed the Tercel, by now engulfed in flames, it exploded with a loud boom, black smoke swirling into the blue sky, debris rocketing up and raining down in all directions.

Chapter Twenty-Eight

10:56 am, Friday, January 6th, Nels' apartment, Costambar.

Eight year old boy killed by stray bullet.

Nels winced as he read details of the story in "El Diario," one of the local papers serving the area.

Yesterday afternoon, as clear as authorities could tell, around 4:44 pm, eight year old Vin Santos died of a single gunshot wound from a stray bullet that penetrated the wooden door of his house and struck him in the heart, killing him instantly. Witnesses say the bullet came from a lone gunman who was the driver of a vehicle apparently in high speed pursuit of another vehicle through a residential neighborhood a few blocks from the Malecon. A police investigation is underway.

Nels noticed the vehicle descriptions weren't even given and he doubted anything would come of the investigation, if there would even be one. Murders happened all the time in the DR, he knew, and were often never solved-or even investigated.

He sipped his coffee at the kitchen table and glanced out the open patio door-another beautiful day in paradise. A strong wind blew through the windows, keeping the temperature nice and cool.

He went through the paper page by page trying to find something about the death of Eduardo, but there was nothing. Authorities had likely discovered the vehicle by now, but the story hadn't gotten to the press-for reasons he would never know.

He had talked to Novelee about an hour ago and she sounded in better spirits. He had decided to mention nothing of his near fatal experience with Eduardo. What was the point anyway? She had enough problems of her own. She had told him she would be working again this afternoon and promised to call him when she got off. Last night, she said she had worked until ten in the evening and then gone out to the Malecon and gotten drunk with her boss.

By her admission, she had managed to polish off about eight or nine Bohemias, had tried to drunk-dial Nels at about three in the morning but his phone had been turned off. She had also tried to catch a motoconcho over to his apartment- to surprise him with a night of passionate lovemaking.

"Many men I met on the Malecon said I was hot," she had said. "And they wanted to go out with me. But I told them all I have a boyfriend and will not stray from him."

"That's good," Nels had said. "I love you," he had also said, unsure if he had meant it. He had promised to call her later.

"Thank god I do turn my phone of at night," he said out loud, wondering what it would have been like to see a wasted Novelee show up on a motoconcho.

He had also spoken to Belinda at about nine in the morning. After the close call yesterday, he had confirmed with Juan he had survived the ordeal but was worried about his friends.

So Juan had called in one of his connections. Belinda and Simon now had an around the clock, armed bodyguard standing outside their door.

Belinda was scared but still hadn't decided if she was going to return home early. Simon, for his part wanted to stay.

There were a lot of things Nels did not know about his friend Juan, but he was sure glad to have him on his side. When he had finally arrived back at Costambar, about nine thirty in the evening, Juan promised him he would be extra vigilant that night.

He had also done something extremely rare for a Dominican. He loaned Nels a loaded hand gun, showed him how to switch the safety on and off, and Nels had slept with it under his pillow last night.

As long as Fabiola was still alive, he still feared for the life of himself and his friends.

"Nels," Juan shouted from the poolside patio. He walked out to the balcony. Juan was washing down the patio with a hose and filling the pool with water. He looked up at Nels and smiled. "How are you doing brother?"

"I'm okay, and you?"

"Good, good, how did you sleep?"

It was a question Juan asked often. Apparently, they were both part-time insomniacs. On a few occasions, Nels had given Juan sleeping pills and Juan had been impressed by the results.

"I slept great," Nels said. "I didn't even need to take any sleeping pills. You?"

"Me too, had a great sleep. No pills."

Juan's phone suddenly rang. He talked for a few minutes and Nels noticed his features darken. After he hung up, he dropped the hose, immediately turned it off, and started hurriedly walking into his apartment.

"What's going on?" Nels asked from the balcony.

"One of my friends was just shot and killed in Santiago. I have to go there right away. Are you going to be okay?"

"Yeah, go," Nels said. "Sorry to hear it. Be safe. Call me when you return."

About an hour and a half later, after he had showered, responded to a few client emails, and had eaten a bowl of cereal with bananas, he sat on the balcony with a rum and water and reflected on his dream last night. He found when he took the sleeping pills he didn't dream-or he couldn't remember them.

But, without the pills, the dreams were lucid and oftentimes terrifying and foretelling.

But last night had been different. After having a few drinks poolside with Juan, he had retreated into his apartment at about 10:30 pm, and promptly drifted off into a deep REM sleep, waking up completely refreshed and rejuvenated.

And his dream had been for the most part pleasing. It was a sunlit day and he was on a tennis court. A slim, dark-haired attractive brunette had walked onto the court. They started conversing and she told Nels that, although not highly ranked, she was a professional tennis player.

A few minutes later Nels was enjoying a spirited rally on the tennis courts with the woman. She was very talented with the ball and he was also impressed with her other talents. Nels had played a lot of tennis in his days, so he found it easy to keep up with her.

He made a point not to deliver any hard backhand or forehand shots. As he remembered it, they just rallied for exercise and weren't concerned with tallying points or serving.

After rallying for a time, the woman announced that she had to go, as she was hungry. "All I've eaten today is a few crackers," she had said. "I'm starving."

It seemed like the perfect window. Nels introduced himself, and offered to buy her dinner. "Sure, she had said, and they walked off the court trying to decide what type of food would be most appetizing.

"How about Chinese, Laura," Nels had asked.

"My name is Lindsey," she said. Although she had evidently taken some small offense, she still smiled. "Remember?"

"I'm sorry," Nels said hoping it wouldn't dampen the rapport he was trying to establish. He was deeply attracted to her.

Then he suddenly woke up and frowned after realizing that Laura was an ex-girlfriend from Vancouver. That relationship hadn't ended harmoniously.

But overall, the dream had left him feeling upbeat, like maybe he had a chance with someone as beautiful and talented as Lindsey in real life.

His phone suddenly rang and snapped him out of his reflection.

"Nels, I need your help," Jonas said.

His heart raced. He had been through so much lately, he instantly feared the worst. And, other than the incident with Wilson, Jonas hadn't been made privy to any of it. "What's wrong?" he asked.

"Nothing serious," Jonas said. "Can we meet at Blackbeards in an hour and discuss it?"

"Sure," Nels said, hanging up the phone. Blackbeards was a well-run hotel, bar, restaurant and legal brothel on beachfront road in Costambar.

Although the DR is rife with hookers, Blackbeards is one of the few places people can go to pay for sex and be confident they will not be robbed-or worse, robbed and murdered. The prices are controlled, apparently the girls are checked weekly for disease, and tourists flock there from all over the world to live out their sexual fantasies and sample the local talent.

Nels didn't hold a morally uptight position on the brothel-after all his father was born in Amsterdam, where prostitution and pot-smoking were completely legal. He had also read that Holland had one of the lowest crime rates in the European continent related to drugs or sex.

So, he wasn't about to declare himself God and start judging those who frequented the brothel.

Besides, the food was inexpensive and delicious and the scenery was nice.

Chapter Twenty-Nine

2:36 pm, Friday, January 6th, Blackbeards, Costambar

"You want me as a witness?" Nels asked Jonas as he took a bite out of his tuna sandwich and watched the shapely bikini-clad Dominican women stroll about the restaurant and lounge poolside with some of the guests.

One male guest was quite wasted and staggered around the premises, smiling and babbling some incomprehensible gibberish to waitresses, hookers, other guests. He had obviously been hit very hard by the Bohemia, Presidente, or Brugal fog. One, or perhaps a combination. Who knew.

But Nels was sure he wouldn't remember anything the following day. And, guaranteed his head would be aching. *Enjoy it while it lasts my friend. You'll pay for it tomorrow.*

"Yes," Jonas said, picking away at his fries. He had ordered a ham and cheese sandwich with fries and a coffee.

For the time being anyway, Nels also drank coffee.

"This morning Irene left for about an hour. She comes back with two large suitcases and brings them into the room. I discover she has about twenty different outfits with her. Then she asks if, when I leave, would I be prepared to pay for the apartment on a monthly basis, to keep her in the luxury she's become accustomed to," Jonas explained.

"That's fucked up," Nels said. "Where is she now?"

"In the apartment. I didn't leave any valuables or cash behind. Only my computer and I'm prepared to lose it."

Nels nodded.

Jonas continued. "I walked the beach today, to clear my head, figure out what I'm going to do. I want her gone and I want you as a witness when I kick her out-to make sure there isn't any drama and I don't end up in trouble with the police."

"I can do that," Nels said, smiling at an attractive hooker who was giving him a friendly look. "Do you have a plan to get rid of her?"

"I've thought of a couple of scenarios. Any ideas?"

Nels thought about it for a few minutes while he finished his tuna sandwich. "How about this: You tell her you have a lot of work to do and you need a few days of total privacy to finish it. Promise to call her in a few days but ask her politely to pack her bags and leave. Offer to call a motoconcho and throw her a thousand pesos, something like that. Make sure you stress that you're very happy with her and want to see her again."

Jonas paused and thought about it while he finished the last of his fries. "You know she eats four meals a day, not to mention her drinking and smoking. I figure she costs me 1,800 pesos in expenses and that's before I pay her 1,000 pesos for sex. I'm better off buying a hooker here for 1,600 pesos, having my fun and being done with it. I don't need all the drama."

Nels nodded as he finished off his meal. The tall, shapely hooker who was giving him the eye walked over and introduced herself. She had long black hair, a beautiful smile and a sexy twinkle in her brown eyes. Her soft facial features were beautiful, her body, slim and perfect. One of her best features was her ample and perfectly shaped breasts. She called herself Baby. She looked about twenty- three years old.

Jonas and Nels engaged in some small talk with her. Jonas inquired about her availability while Nels politely told her he had a girlfriend and he would like some time to get caught up with his friend. She smiled and left the table.

"I like your plan," Jonas finally said. "Let's go activate it. You know I went to her house the other day, just to see how she lives. It's a humble abode, but a clean Christian household. I gave her about eight hundred pesos to give to her parents and her two teenage kids. You know how much she gave them?"

"Nothing?" Nels asked.

"Close. She gave each of the kids twenty five pesos, gave her mother nothing, and you wouldn't believe how disrespectful she talked to her mother."

"I'm starting to think I would believe," Nels said.

A few minutes later, they walked back to Villas Lirio, along the road that fronted the beach. Nels looked out at the ocean and thought of the idyllic advertisements he had seen promoting the DR beaches as a relaxing paradise on earth.

If this was paradise, he thought, *there was trouble in paradise*. And, at some point, he knew he would have to warn his friend about the danger still lurking in the shadows.

Chapter Thirty

4:00 pm, Friday, January 6th, Villas Lirio, Costambar, apartment number three.

Jonas knew when to take an opportunity and run with it. When they had arrived back to the apartment, Irene had prepared dinner-pasta and pork chops-and it sat on the kitchen counter getting cold.

They found her sitting on the bed, a little pout creasing her small features.

"I have a toothache," she said sadly.

Nels just happened to have a business card for a Dominican dentist in his pocket. If he had time, he had planned on getting a few repairs done to his teeth, as well as a cleaning. He knew from experience, the dentist he had in mind had done an admirable job for some of his friends and the cost was about one third the price of Canadian dentists.

"Oh, you poor thing," Jonas said, feigning deep concern. She stood up and he hugged her. "Listen, you should really get that looked at." He pulled out a five hundred peso note and handed it to her.

On cue, Nels produced the business card from his pocket, handing it to her. She looked at it blankly and took it.

Jonas explained to her in very good and diplomatic Spanish what the situation was. When he finished, she sat down and started crying. Not many tears dropped.

"It's not only you Irene, it's me as well," Nels said, trying to soften the blow. "As soon as you leave, he wants me gone, and we're best friends. He needs absolute and total privacy to complete his work."

Irene stared at Nels, trying to read his level of sincerity. Her doubtful expression said she wasn't buying it, but nor was she prepared to call him on it.

Nels and Jonas walked out of the bedroom and sat down on the white plastic chairs on the small main floor patio. Nels looked at the still water in the small swimming pool and wondered if any of the tenants actually used it.

"Call the motoconcho," Jonas said.

Nels got Daniel on the phone and explained a woman with a few suitcases would soon need a lift home.

"I'll be there in ten minutes," Daniel said and hung up.

Nels sub-consciously crossed his fingers. "When Daniel arrives, I'll go outside the gates and see her off with you. Before he takes off, I'll walk away, make like I'm going home, leaving you to your work. When I see the motoconcho gone, I'll make a U-turn," Nels explained in English knowing Irene couldn't understand a word of it.

Jonas nodded and smiled.

Ten minutes later, Irene had her bags packed and stood curbside, about to climb aboard the motoconcho. Jonas hugged and kissed her, promising to call in a few days.

Nels gave her a hug and walked down the street. As he watched the motoconcho speed out of sight, he wiped his brow, which had collected a few beads of sweat.

So much of the underlying motivation behind Dominican friendliness was motivated by a desire for money, he thought. But, it was still nice to see that scenario unfold with very little drama.

He turned around and walked back to Villas Lirio.

He doubted any future scenarios would unfold with so little drama. And, he decided no time like the present to warn his good friend about the potential danger ahead.

Chapter Thirty-One

7:55 pm, Saturday, January 7th, Monument to the heroes of the Restoration, Santiago, DR.

A silver Ford Explorer was parked in front of the popular tourist attraction, which offered a panoramic view of the city when you reached the top of the stairs. Originally commissioned by dictator Rafael Leonidas Trujillo in 1944 as a peace monument to honor him, after his assassination in 1961, the government changed the name to honor the heroes in the war against Spanish colonist forces.

Through his binoculars, Javier could see Fabiola approaching what looked to be a foreign tourist at the base of the monument.

They conversed for a few minutes, then the tourist hailed a cab, and they both got in and sped away.

Javier noticed a black four door sedan pull out and follow the pair. He pulled out, but kept his distance, following both vehicles.

He smiled to himself. *Two for the price of one.* He liked killing when he was righting a wrong.

Javier wasn't a very big man, but he was quick. He was ex-military and still worked for the Puerto Plata police force. He stood about 5 foot 7 inches, weighing in at a slender and muscular 170 pounds. He sported a black mustache, but was otherwise always clean shaven. His black hair was always neatly cropped close to his scalp-the tennis ball look. He didn't go more than two weeks without getting a haircut and he was meticulous about his clothes.

On this day he wore rugged black hiking boots, neatly pressed blue jeans and a black button up shirt with a collar, also neatly ironed.

He had sharp, small brown eyes. His friendly demeanor could change on a dime and he was capable of extreme violence-in fact he thrived on it.

He pushed weights daily, was strict with his diet, did not smoke and only indulged in alcohol occasionally. He liked his whiskey neat, and sometimes he would drink just enough to get a glow on.

But, he would not permit himself to get shit-faced. To do that, would mean letting his guard down. And when you lived on the edge like Javier, it was not a smart thing to do.

Most of the contracts he took involved killing bad people. But, if he had to be completely honest with himself, he had killed a few good ones in the mix.

But, he didn't enjoy it when he had to kill a good person. He only did it to supplement his meager police salary. He was in the middle of constructing a house for himself, his wife and three kids in Puerto Plata. There were always a few cost over-runs that sometimes involved taking contracts he would perhaps otherwise turn down.

He justified it by killing many of the thieves he caught in Puerto Plata. In his mind, he was making the city a better place for tourists, and by extension more economically viable.

Sometimes he would just shoot them with his handgun.

Other times, if he was in a bad mood, he would slash them up with either his machete or hunting knife, whichever one he felt like practicing with at the time.

He kept his handgun polished at all times, his cutlery, clean and razor sharp. He was methodical and not about to leave anything to chance.

He noticed the taxi pull up at the Mar y Sol Hotel in downtown Santiago. Fabiola and the long-haired foreign male exited the car and walked into the hotel, arm in arm.

The black car parked a short distance away. The driver stayed inside.

Javier didn't waste any time. He parked about a block down from the black car, pulled the silencer out of the glove box and fastened it to his handgun. He loosened his shirt, tucked the piece into his crotch, and pulled out a cigarette from a pack in the glove box.

He approached the vehicle from the passenger side, the smoke dangling from his mouth, smiling, knocking on the window, and motioning to the driver for a light.

The man hesitated, but only for a moment, before rolling down the window. For his trouble, he was shot once in the head. His brains blew out the back of his head onto the driver side window, and he slumped over.

"Aaahhhhhh" was the only word Javier heard coming from the now dead man's mouth as he walked away from the vehicle and into the hotel.

He flashed his police badge to the female receptionist and she immediately provided the room number for Ben, the American tourist. He gave her a stern warning to keep her mouth shut, before taking the elevator up to the fourth floor.

Javier's influence was far-reaching and once she heard the name, he knew she would be too scared to open her mouth. *This is too easy*, he thought to himself, grinning as he walked down the hall to room 404. Of course, it made it even easier that Fabiola was wanted by the police on numerous charges, including murder.

Not that they were really looking for her, but she was wanted none-the-less.

Javier didn't waste any time kicking the door in. It flew open and he saw Ben already buck naked, legs and arms outstretched, tied to the bed and gagged. His eyes bulged open with fear.

Fabiola stood beside him with her cell phone in hand. She was topless with only a red G-string on, and long black boots. Her large breasts bounced as she ducked the first shot, reaching for a small pistol in her boot.

She pulled it out and fired, but Javier had already raced into the room, dove and fired another shot at her trigger hand. It blew her trigger finger clean off and she dropped the piece with a small scream.

She bent to retrieve it with her good hand but he was already upon her and kicked her flush in the jaw, just as she reached for her gun.

She screamed again, the force of the blow toppling her into a nightstand beside the bed. She smashed into it and the lamp toppled, the bulb breaking with a pop.

Javier advanced toward her with rapid speed, pulling out his hunting knife and slashing a large x on her belly. Her intestines spilled out and blood drained onto her body. She instinctively put her hands to her belly, trying to contain her internal organs.

Ben moaned and his eyes grew wider as he watched the carnage.

Javier winked at him and with a swift fluid motion slashed Fabiola's jugular vein. Her right hand reached for her throat, blood spurted from her mouth and she collapsed on the floor, the pool of blood rapidly becoming a small pond.

Javier approached Ben with the knife and the young hippie screamed through his gag, a muffled sound.

Javier put an index finger to his mouth and Ben became quiet.

He quickly cut the cloth pieces constraining the man's extremities, removed the gag, turned and left the room. He had no idea if the man understood Spanish but it was the only language he knew.

"Someone will be in to clean this mess up very soon. Put on your clothes and relax."

Ben just nodded, too afraid to question anything. He didn't understand a single word Javier was saying but he was in no condition to argue. Besides, this man had just saved his life.

"Gracious," he said, one of the very few Spanish words he knew.

Javier smiled, wiped his blade clean on the sheet covers, and left. On the way down the hall, he plucked his cell phone from his pocket and called his connection at the Santiago Police Department.

"I've just done your job for you," he said when the man picked up. "Room 404 Mar y Sol and black four door sedan parked in front. Come and clean this mess up. You owe me a bottle of whiskey."

"Yes," the policeman said and hung up the phone.

Chapter Thirty-Two

11:01 pm, Saturday, January 7th, small apartment in middle class neighborhood, Santiago, DR.

Juan was examining his bullet-ridden friend Amirilis when the call came in.

"Hello," he said, instantly recognizing the number. He wouldn't say the name in mixed company, however.

Melina still hugged her dead boyfriend, sobbing.

"It's done," Javier said. "They won't be giving your friends any more trouble. Let me know if you have any more work."

"Thanks," Juan said, realizing Javier had already hung up the phone. He wasn't into a lot of small talk.

Juan had arrived at the apartment a few minutes ago and was just now learning the story.

Amarilis lay slumped on the bed, two bullets in his chest and one in his head. His mouth was wide open, a panicked expression distorting his otherwise handsome features.

Melina was beside him on the bed, hugging him, kissing his cheek and sobbing.

"Please," Juan finally said after a few minutes, taking her arm and lifting her up gently. She wrapped her arms around him in an embrace, and sobbed against his muscular chest. Her deep brown eyes were bloodshot from crying and her white blouse and parts of her long black hair were stained with Amarilis' blood. "I need to get the story from you."

She finally stopped crying, pulled herself away from the embrace and sat down in a chair beside the bed.

Juan went into the bathroom, extracted some toilet paper from a roll beside the toilet, returned and handed it to her. She thanked him, and began wiping away her tears.

"Have you called the police yet?" Juan asked.

"No, we called you, only."

"I'll look after that," he said. "Now tell me the story."

Melina explained that they were in the apartment together, earlier in the day, and she had left to pick up some chicken, beans and rice to go. Returning with the take-out food about fifteen minutes later, she heard gunshots coming from the apartment. Too scared to enter, she had ducked into a stairwell.

About thirty seconds later, she saw a Dominican male leave the room and run down the hallway, heading to the far exit. She gave a description of the man to Juan. She had also seen him before and gave Juan the location of the neighborhood he hung around.

The motivation had been money. About five thousand pesos were missing from the apartment, all her silver jewelry and a laptop computer.

Juan had pulled out a small steno pad, and took notes as she spoke. He looked at the body again. From the disheveled state of the apartment, and the marks on Amarilis' arms, it looked like he had resisted-a decision he had paid for with his life.

"Do you know if he's a member of Los Perros?" he asked. Los Perros was the name of a street gang that operated in the city of Santiago.

"I don't think so," she said. "I've seen him before, and I believe he operates alone."

Juan knew once he obtained the name of the man, he could quickly and easily ascertain from his connections if the killer was a gang member. He wanted to be sure, before he went after him, that he wouldn't open up a potentially lethal can of worms.

"Stay here," he instructed her. "The police and ambulance will arrive shortly to clean this up. Don't worry, with time, everything will be okay."

Juan hugged Melina a final time and left the apartment. He wasn't in a very good mood. He had been friends with Amarilis for over ten years, and the man was as honest and loyal as they came. The two had been very close and his death had left Juan feeling hollow, empty and sad.

Juan wouldn't enjoy killing the killer. It was not something he liked doing. But he knew it would make him feel a little better knowing he had avenged the death of one of his best friends.

It would also give him some satisfaction in the knowledge that he was cleaning out the trash in Santiago, a city already known for being one of the cleanest in the country.

Chapter Thirty-Three

1:33 am, Sunday, January 8th, seedy residential district, Santiago, DR.

A blue untraceable Toyota Camry was parked outside a run-down apartment building. Juan sat in the driver's seat and waited. He pulled out his handgun, wiped it with a small white cloth, checked the chamber, removed the safety, and tucked it back into the crotch area of his jeans.

It hadn't taken him long to learn that the killer, Miguel, was not a member of Los Perros, and he operated alone as a petty thief. Asking around the neighborhood, he was also quick to ascertain Miguel's address and learn he had recently been estranged from his wife and kids. Evidently he had a temper and some anger management issues that needed addressing. He was prone to extreme violence when he drank. And, from what Juan had learned on the streets, he drank a lot.

He lived alone in a one room apartment with only a bathroom. His only means of income was stealing; and if that resulted in the odd murder-so be it. Apparently, Miguel didn't have a conscience.

And, he didn't have a girlfriend, either, so that would make Juan's work a lot easier.

Juan had contemplated hiring Javier to do the work-but he was a little tight for cash right now. The small apartment building he owned needed some repairs and two of the vacant units had to be fixed up a little before he would be able to rent them out. He made a point of renting to foreigners only. He had made a few errors in judgement by renting to Dominicans in the past and had learned from his mistakes.

He had rented a two bedroom unit to a middle aged couple with no kids. Three days later, he discovered about twelve people living in the apartment, including about five kids. They partied loudly almost every day from dusk to dawn and caused a lot of damage to the unit. Evicting them had been easy-especially when they were staring down the business end of a handgun.

Juan saw a small man staggering down the street toward the apartment. He looked a little-if not a lot-drunk. He waited until the man passed underneath the streetlamp to get a better view-it was Miguel alright.

Juan made a snap decision to take him out on the street. A few dogs barked and some faint Bachata music thumped out from a house halfway down the block. But otherwise, the streets were quiet and barren.

Juan ducked while Miguel passed his vehicle. He opened the door and ran toward him. He stopped about six feet behind Miguel, leveling his gun and firing at the back of his head.

Miguel had already ducked, drawn his weapon and returned fire.

The bullet narrowly missed Juan's head-by a stroke of luck-and he quickly tucked his piece away and tackled the small man, sending him hard to the pavement, knocking the gun from his hand.

Evidently one of Miguel's friends whom Juan had questioned had tipped the killer off. The drunk act was a fake.

But Miguel was no match for Juan's strength. Juan wrestled with him on the ground for a few seconds before pinning him down. He pulled out his gun, pointed it at his chest-Miguel had put his hands to his face- and fired it three times-pop-pop-pop.

Miguel winced in pain, gasped for breath twice, and his body went limp.

A symphony of dog barks echoed through the street-roop-roop-roop-roop-roop.

A car alarm went of-beeeeep-beeeeeep-beeeeeep-beeeeeeep-waaaah-waaaah-waaaah-waaaah-waaaah.

Juan ran to his vehicle-started it in an instant-and squealed away.

For someone who is trying to live a tranquil life, he thought, *I'm certainly getting my fair share of drama.*

Chapter Thirty-Four

2:45pm, Monday, January 9th, Nels' apartment, Costambar.

Nels sat on his balcony drinking a Bohemia, waiting for the arrival of Novelee. He wondered what kind of drama would unfold on this day.

He saw Juan pull up to the curb of the apartment in a new gold Explorer-he had seen the man pull up in about five different types of vehicles since his arrival. He knew Juan was also involved in a car rental business-so that shouldn't be any surprise-but he suspected there were other reasons for changing vehicles.

He also knew he would never ask the question.

Juan walked up the stairs leading to the apartment with his girlfriend, Oria. They both smiled at him from below.

"How do you feel, little brother?" Juan asked.

"I feel good," Nels replied.

"Are you sure? You feel good?" Juan was unlike a lot of people Nels knew-when he asked how you were feeling, he really wanted to know how you were feeling.

"I feel good," Nels said. "And you?"

"Good, very good. I have some news for you. I'll come over later, if that's okay?"

"Of course it is. Come over for a beer." Nels tipped his bottle up and took a swig.

"To your health," Juan said, entering the building with Oria.

Nels looked out at the peak-a-boo ocean view and contemplated his dream last night.

Or was it a nightmare?

He was walking through the streets of Costambar and people-lots of them-approached him asking for money.

Some were Dominicans-and still others were foreigners.

He started by handing them one hundred peso notes. Some were satisfied with the amounts, while others wanted more.

He kept handing out the money until he suddenly realized he had very little of it left in his pocket-and he felt very hungry.

He had asked himself, "What the fuck am I doing anyway?"

He started saying no to the crowds of people with their hands out and some of them had become angry. That's when he started running. Before long, he was being pursued through the streets by an angry mob, yelling and screaming and intent on getting their hands on what little money he had left.

And, of course, he couldn't find his apartment. He remembered thinking of Juan in the nightmare. If he could find his apartment, he had reasoned, he could find Juan. And Juan would protect him.

There was a knock at the door.

"Little brother, it's me," Juan said, behind the door.

Nels opened it and Juan stepped inside, beaming. He gave Nels a big bear hug, and then looked at him with concern.

"You sleeping okay?" he asked.

"Yes, I am." In fact, Nels had spent last night partying on the beach with Jonas, and the night before he had invited Belinda and Simon to the beach to join him for a relaxing day swimming. They had decided to stay and had visited Nels via taxi, arranged by Juan's bodyguard.

He had talked to Novelee on both nights and she had informed him she had to work late at the manicure salon, but she promised to come over today. And, apparently she was on her way over now-albeit on Dominican time, which would probably be two hours later than when she had said.

But Nels was in no hurry to see her-it was the little general who didn't have a lot of patience.

"And you?" he asked Juan.

"Not so well. I stayed in Santiago last night, but didn't get a lot of sleep."

"Before you leave, I'll give you two more Zoplicones, the ones you say work well for you."

"Okay," Juan said. "Thank you."

Nels walked into the kitchen, cracked open a large bottle of Bohemia with a spoon-he had no bottle opener- poured Juan a glass and the two sat out on the balcony, enjoying the afternoon sun.

Nels would not ask about Juan's business in Santiago-he suspected he was avenging the death of a friend-and knew the less he knew the healthier he would be.

"To your health," Juan said, holding up his glass.

Nels clinked it. "To your health."

"I have some good news," Juan said.

"Go ahead."

"The Fabiola problem has been solved. I think I can call off the bodyguard for your friends"

"That's great," Nels said, without a shred of emotion. "Is there anyone else we need to be concerned about?"

"I don't think so, not on my end anyway."

"What does that mean?" Nels asked.

"Well, I didn't know how to say this to you earlier-we didn't know each other that well before- but now that we've become close I think I should warn you."

"About what?" Nels asked.

"Novelee. I don't trust her. And I don't think she's good for you."

"Funny, I've been thinking the same thing."

"She's poor, uneducated and probably jobless. Who knows how long she'll be at that job."

Nels had filled Juan in previously on a few of his hunches about Novelee and it appeared the man was adding things up.

Juan continued, after pausing to take a swig of his beer. "I think you'll have nothing but problems with her. And I think she's after your money. And, I wouldn't believe half the stories she says about why she needs the money. You need someone smart, educated and employed, preferably with no kids."

"You're probably right," Nels said. "But I might cut this trip short and I'm not in the mood for any more drama before I leave. Maybe when I leave, I'll just never call her again."

"Suit yourself," Juan said, a questioning expression on his face.

Nels could tell he didn't agree with the plan but had decided not to push the matter.

Juan took another drink of his beer. It was almost finished so Nels walked to the fridge, removed the half full bottle, returned and refilled both glasses.

"I have someone else I'd like you to meet," Juan said, after Nels had sat down.

"Who?"

"My girlfriend's sister. Her name is Cara. She's studying to be a teacher at the university and she has a full time job working for the phone company in Santiago."

"How old is she?"

"Twenty four," Juan said. "And she has no kids, an awesome personality, her own apartment and a vehicle."

Nels couldn't help but wonder how much better a relationship might be if he could meet an educated, gainfully employed, Dominican woman.

"How does she look?" Nels asked.

"She's beautiful," he said, describing her figure by curving his hands and arms in the air.

"Any pictures?" Nels asked.

"I have some in my computer. Come up and have a look."

"Some other time," Nels said. "Novelee's on her way over."

Chapter Thirty-Five

4:30 pm, Monday, January 9th, Pascual's beach restaurant and bar, Costambar.

"I'm going to kill her," Novelee said, as she sipped her fruit juice.

She was talking about her female boss at the manicure salon, where she had worked for the last three days. She complained that for three days work, the owner had only paid her 1,200 pesos. Nels quickly figured the math out for a month's work. It added up to $263.16 US, more than the average monthly Dominican salary.

"Kill her?" he asked.

"Yeah, I'm going to kill her. You know I threatened to kick the shit out of her on my last day there."

Nels doubted she would be calling her anytime soon for more work. "And how did she respond?"

"With fear," Novelee said, matter-of-factly. "She's afraid of me, you know."

Nels stared out at the ocean and wondered where the conversation would turn next.

"I like those sandals, and that shirt," Novelee said.

He was wearing a black button up short sleeve shirt, green knee length shorts with plenty of pockets, and brown leather flip-flop sandals. "Thanks," he said.

"Not like the clothes you brought the last time you were here. They were ugly."

"Thanks again for your interest," Nels said, grimacing. He wasn't in the mood for a fight. Not today, anyway.

"Well it's true. Would you rather I not tell you the truth?"

Pick your battles, Nels thought. In spite of the criticism he was receiving, her low cut top exposed plenty of cleavage, and her mini-skirt left little to the imagination. He wanted to get her into the bedroom. And soon.

Men can be such fools, he thought. The little general always doing the thinking and, in his case commanding the troops well behind enemy lines. He doubted he could bring them out without a few battle scars, or without being completely shell-shocked.

He decided to change the subject. "How is your throat doing with the new medication?"

"I'm feeling better," she said. "I think it's working."

"That's good news," he said, thinking he could no longer blame her mood swings and ill temper on the thyroid condition.

"Yes," she said, smiling. She bent over and kissed him on the lips.

"The lovebirds," Jonas said, approaching their table on the sand. He wore swimming trunks and was dripping wet from a dip in the ocean. He carried a small knapsack, from which he pulled out a towel, dried himself and sat down beside them.

Novelee's demeanor changed instantly. Her face lit up with a big smile. She offered Jonas a warm hug, and he pecked her on the cheek.

A waitress came over and he ordered a large Bohemia and a menu.

"How's everything?" he asked Nels in English. Nels was happy for the company, someone he could talk to reasonably and intelligently-and in English for a change.

"It's great," Nels said. "I'll fill you in on some details later."

Nels had briefed him on the Fabiola problem and he knew Jonas was anxious to learn how things turned out.

They called it the F problem, to keep Novelee out of the loop. "The F problem is solved," Nels said with a smile.

The waitress arrived and poured some beer into their glasses. They toasted. Novelee clinked her fruit juice, although she had no clue as to what they were celebrating.

"That's good," Jonas said. "So you think we're in the clear?"

"I hope so," Nels said. "But I think I'm going to cut my trip short, leave around the end of the month. I just don't feel up to handling three months after everything that's happened. And there's someone else I want to get rid of," he said, discreetly pointing to his left where Novelee sat.

He made a point of feigning interest in some boat in the ocean at the same time, knowing she was adept at reading facial expressions. She might not know the language, but she could often tell from gestures, tone of voice, facial expressions and eye contact if someone was speaking badly about her.

Nels had made the mistake before and wasn't about to make it again.

"I understand," Jonas said, smiling at Novelee. She smiled back.

"I might have another job," she said.

"Oh," Jonas asked.

"I applied for a job in on the Semana peninsula, there's a new hotel that just opened up, and they need waitresses. I got a call the other day. They want me to come for an interview."

"That's great," Jonas said. "When are you leaving?"

"I'm stalling them until Nels leaves. Once he leaves, I'll leave the next day."

Suddenly, it clouded over and the rain came-it was a torrential downpour. They rushed inside the restaurant for cover and took their seats. The waitress came over again and they all ordered food and drinks-Novelee also ordered a large Bohemia, saying she wanted to celebrate the fact her thyroid condition had improved.

They watched the rain, ate and drank. Little rivers formed on the bumpy dirt beachfront road.

"You know, everyone talks about the predatory nature of the women in the DR," Jonas said, pointing to the little rivers of water to distract Novelee. She followed his finger, looking at the rivers blankly. "What about the men? I've heard a few stories about Dominican men, even foreigners praying on foreign women and sapping them of every penny they have."

"I've heard a few stories myself," Nels agreed. "A Canadian friend of mine moved to Cabarete a few years ago with about $200,000 in investments, thinking she would retire in paradise. Well, she met a foreigner, European I believe, and he took her for almost every nickel in two years. She later got sick and died in her apartment. She weighed next to nothing when she died, and apparently the man wouldn't even take her to the hospital. Can you believe that? My heart goes out to Melanie. She was one of my dearest friends and I loved her."

"I've heard that story before," Jonas said. "And I've heard stories of a few young Dominican men meeting older foreign women and taking them for their money."

"Such a crazy place," Nels said, smiling at Novelee and giving her a quick kiss on the lips. "Aren't they called Sankees?"

"Sankees," Jonas agreed, watching Novelee's eyebrows raise at the Spanish word. Fortunately her meal had arrived and her mouth was full of chicken. Nels knew only too well, she didn't like to talk while eating.

Chapter Thirty-Six

1:36 pm, Tuesday, January 10th, Nels' apartment, poolside, Costambar.

"I think this place changes people," Belinda observed, sipping a Cuba libre and watching Simon swim laps.

They lounged in bed-style plastic patio chairs. Nels also sported a Cuba libre.

It was a hot, clear, sunny day with very little wind.

Simon wasn't much of drinker but Belinda and Nels seemed intent on tying one on. Last night, Nels, Novelee and Jonas had been stuck in the beach bar zone until about 10:00 pm, by the time the rain had let up.

So, without a better plan, they had hopped from beach bar to beach bar-starting at Pascual's, then Selecta, then the Happy Hippo and finally El Caribe. By the time the rain had stopped all three were very drunk.

And, for a change, it was a night with very little drama. The drunker Novelee became, the more affectionate she got with Nels. By the time, they staggered home, she couldn't keep her hands off him.

Jonas had walked with them a little ways, then veered off for a little business at Blackbeards, while Nels took Novelee home and had a pretty enjoyable love making session of his own.

She woke up cranky and with a pounding headache. Luckily, her cousin called her first thing in the morning saying she had to go to work and little Papito was playing in the street. Come and deal with your kid.

So Novelee had left, early but not before complaining to Nels that she was very surprised when her parents left to live in the country, that they didn't take little Papito with them to look after him. She said that while she was married to the German who had incarcerated her in his house, she had given them plenty of money and expected something in return.

Nels didn't feel her parents owed her anything, but nodded his head, knowing full well that many Dominican women dump their kids off on their parents after giving birth so they could pursue, well, whatever really interested them.

"I would have to agree with that," Nels finally said, processing the information through a thick fog. Belinda had begun to look at him strangely. "I know when I return, I won't be the same. But I've seen it also change people in bad ways. A friend of mine, Bill, came down here a few years ago from Canada, for a three month stay. By the end of the first week, he was getting drunk, dusk to dawn every day, and he had turned into an obnoxious asshole. Made a number of errors in judgement, and I saw him giving a lot of people shit, like really freaking out on them, for no reason. He even made one woman cry with his insults."

"That's terrible," Belinda said. "But I think for the DR to change people like that they have to be fucked up even before they get here. Bill must have had a lot of problems back home that he brought down here."

"I hope that never happens to me," Nels said.

"It won't," she said. "You're not fucked up. You're a good guy, with good morals. If anything it will change you for the better."

"Thanks," he said. "Maybe Bill just got tired of people ripping him off and became cynical, his judgement, skewed by all the booze."

"Who knows, but I doubt it," Belinda countered.

Nels knew one thing- when he returned to Canada he would sleep like a baby- pill free-in his own bed. And, he looked forward to getting off the booze for awhile. It seemed more and more that events and dates were getting harder and harder to remember. And he had been here less than a month.

Imagine if he lived here.

Simon popped out of the pool, taking deep breaths and smiling. He had just completed twenty laps. "I need a beer," he said, walking over to the cooler that Belinda had bought on the way in from Puerto Plata.

Juan and Oria walked out and greeted them, just as Simon had toweled off, cracked a beer and reclined on one of the patio chairs.

"How's the water?" he asked Simon. Juan loved seeing his tenants and guests enjoying the pool. He spent so much time cleaning and maintaining it.

Nels translated and Simon said, "Great."

"Want one?" Nels asked them. They both nodded. Nels picked two Bohemias from the cooler, cracked them open with his spoon-he still hadn't bothered to buy a bottle opener- and handed one to Oria, the other to Juan.

Walking back to his seat, he suddenly veered off and dove in the pool, making a big-belly flop- splash. It was the first time he had been swimming since his arrival.

Juan smiled and Oria laughed. Even Simon and Belinda smiled, enjoying Nels enjoying himself for a change.

"Will you to look at something on my Skype?" Juan asked Nels, after he had popped out of the pool and toweled himself dry. "I'm having a problem with one of the features."

Nels thought he knew what his friend was up to. "I'll be right back," he said to his friends. Oria took a seat beside Simon and Belinda and smiled.

The more Nels got to know her, the more he liked her. She was studying medicine at the Puerto Plata University, worked in a bank and came from a middle class Dominican family. She was typically quiet, but if you engaged her in conversation, her words and thoughts were quite intelligent. When she smiled, her whole face lit up and it was infectious.

She actually spoke a little English so they might manage some basic conversation while Nels was upstairs looking at pictures of her sister, Cara.

Upstairs, Juan flipped through images on his computer while Nels admired them. Cara was indeed attractive. She had full, pouty lips, attractive brown eyes, olive-toned skin and perfect white teeth. Her infectious smile reminded Nels of Oria. If there was anything to criticize, perhaps it was her nose. It was just slightly bigger than what Nels would consider the perfect nose for a woman.

But her shapely body more than compensated for it. And, besides, no one was perfect anyway.

Juan smiled as he flipped through the photos, noticing the expression of approval on Nels' face. "What do you think?" he asked.

"She looks every attractive. But, as I said, I don't want to meet anyone until I see this thing through with Novelee-however it turns out."

Juan frowned slightly, and then his normal, cheerful smile returned.

"Which reminds me," Nels said. "Could you do me a little favor?"

"Name it," Juan said.

In recent days, Nels had noticed small sums of money missing from his money pouch-on his last count 2,500 pesos had gone missing from what he was sure was 5,500 pesos that he had counted out and put in the very back of the pouch-which he had tucked under his mattress.

As well, lately he had begun to think about the small netbook that had grown a pair of legs and walked out of his apartment. The more he thought about it, the more he was not prepared to take Novelee off the suspect list.

How could he? He knew she needed money. And he also knew there was some mutual acknowledgement building between the two of them that the relationship wasn't working.

And he remembered how her eyes had lit up just after he had arrived-when she first saw the little netbook. Noticing Nels had two computers, she had mentioned she wanted one just like it, even asking Nels if he even needed it. Nels had assured her he needed both computers.

Nels had also noticed a dramatic shift in Novelee's trust level after he had dumped her for three or four days and then decided to call her. On a few occasions after the big blow-off, she had accused him of not loving her-saying she felt that after he left the DR he would never come back to see her.

And, Nels had to admit, he had been thinking those things.

Whatever the reason, Novelee was not the same person he had known in the DR a year ago. She had become much angrier, short-tempered and negative than he ever remembered her being in the past. As well, her affection for him had decreased noticeably and Nels was aware he had brought a lot of it on himself.

But, he wasn't yet prepared to trash Novelee's reputation in Costambar.

Nels was deep in thought when Juan touched his arm. "You wanted a favor?" Juan asked.

"Yeah," he said. "Could you look into Novelee's connections-see if she's tied in with anybody who could harm or rob me or my friends?" Nels thought of Novelee spending a few days in jail for assaulting her sister and he was now unsure to what depths she was capable of going, to exact what she viewed as revenge.

If he had to be completely honest, he was beginning to fear her.

"Sure, no problem," Juan said.

"But, please, do it discreetly," Nels cautioned.

Juan smiled, putting his hand on Nels' shoulder. "Don't worry little brother. No one will ever know. Now go enjoy yourself with your friends."

"Oh," Nels suddenly remembered as he left Juan's apartment. "Do you want your gun back?"

"Keep it for now. You might need it."

Chapter Thirty-Seven

7:56 pm, Friday the 13th, Nels' apartment, Costambar.

Nels sat on his balcony, sipping a rum punch, examining the full moon. The craters on it formed the image of a smile-no, a laugh. The full moon was laughing at him.

Novelee had been busy the last two days-working and looking after her son, according to her- and it had freed Nels up to relax and enjoy the remainder of his time here. But, she was on her way over and would be arriving soon.

Belinda and Simon's relationship had developed some friction and the two had decided to return to Calgary. Nels had noticed one night having dinner with them that Belinda's patience level with Simon and his wandering eyes had grown thin. It was manifesting itself in nit-picky arguments.

"I told you to put the mushrooms in the salad, not cook them with the steak," she had said as Simon helped her cook dinner.

"There's plenty of mushrooms for both the steak and the salad," he had responded, mild annoyance creasing his handsome features.

"No there isn't," Belinda had said crossly. "Look, there are hardly any mushrooms in the salad."

"There's enough," Simon had responded.

Nels, well on his way to getting drunk, had tried to diffuse the situation. "I can think of better things to argue about than mushrooms," he had said.

They had both laughed suddenly. "If that's all we argue about, I don't think our relationship is that bad," had been Belinda's response.

Juan had driven them to the airport yesterday afternoon and Nels had gone along for the ride. He couldn't help looking over his shoulder on the trip and he noticed his palms were sweating. They arrived at the airport and Nels had hugged them, kissing Belinda on the cheek.

"I love both you guys," he had said, watching them walk through security after receiving their boarding passes.

When they had cleared security, he was finally able to relax, even more this morning, since he had received an email from Belinda saying they had arrived safely.

Nels had yet to hear anything from Juan regarding Novelee's connections-he was almost too afraid to ask. He had begun to drink more, knowing full well it was a coping mechanism for the stress he was feeling-and not really giving a shit one way or the other.

Jonas had become somewhat bored with Costambar and Blackbeards and had decided to spend a few days in the Sewer-potentially rancid waters-but waters Jonas viewed as much more challenging and adventurous to navigate. Nels knew his history with the Sewer-he would probably take a hooker in the morning, one in the late afternoon, and pick one up at the disco late in the evening.

Or he would gather phone numbers at the disco-if he felt it was dangerous- and call the best ones the following afternoon. Jonas viewed the Sewer as an amusement park with adult rides. And he loved the lack of laws that made it possible to have so many adventures.

Nels knew it was Friday the 13th and a full moon to boot, but it didn't really bother him. Someone had once told him the Chinese viewed it as a lucky day and he had long ago decided to adopt the same perception.

If you think bad things, bad things will happen, he often told himself.

His phone rang. It was Jonas. "How's life in the gutter?" Nels asked. "Have you abandoned your morality yet?"

"No, not yet," Jonas said. "If I ever do, please shoot me."

Remembering the handgun tucked underneath his mattress, Nels didn't find the joke funny.

"What are you up to?" Jonas asked.

"Just having a rum punch and waiting for Novelee to show up. And you?"

"I'm taking a break right now-waiting for round three. I picked up some food bacteria, eating some chicken on the beach and I'm paying for it now. I took some Imodium. I hope it holds."

Nels had heard some nasty stories of poisonous spiders, even more deadly centipedes and parasites that had killed-or severely injured-people in the DR. One friend of his had been bitten by a poisonous spider-or a centipede-he wasn't sure, and in a drunken moment had decided to burn the poison out with some gun powder and fire, finally dousing it with alcohol. Two years later the poison had begun creeping back up his leg and Canadian doctors were stymied on how to treat it.

Still another Canadian tourist had received a spider bite sitting on the beach and had to have a large chunk of his calf muscle cut out to stop the spread of the poison. And, if the treatment hadn't been immediate, he probably would have died.

And that's only the bugs-never mind all the tropical diseases floating around that could be potentially fatal.

"I hope it's just the common bacteria," Nels said. "If it is you'll be fine by tomorrow."

"It feels like it," Jonas said. "It's my own stupidity. I spend all this money for a plane ticket to get here. I have a choice between what I know to be good, clean, healthy food, or a cheap chicken dish for 200 pesos. Instead of eating the good stuff, I decide to take a chance. Never again."

Nels was familiar with this mistake. Usually when he travelled to third world countries, he would pay a little more for his restaurant meals, slowly letting his system adjust to the bacteria. After a month or so, if he was feeling adventurous, he would begin to experiment with cheaper restaurants.

In a drunken stupor, he occasionally made the same mistake-and usually paid for it. Luckily on this trip, touch wood-he patted his head-he had not encountered the nasty stomach bacteria.

"I met a retired Swedish guy yesterday," Jonas said. "And he took me to his luxurious house on the beach, a few minutes outside Sosua."

"What did you think?" Nels asked.

"Well, he's retired down here, about 63 years old, and lives in this well-guarded gated fortress. His life consists of going to the beach in the late morning, bringing a hooker back in the late afternoon, and then going to bed before nine thirty at night."

"Does he have health problems?"

"I don't know, he must have, but he didn't mention anything. Just, after his hooker adventures he's too tired to do anything. He showed me the house, wanted to rent it to me for $2,000 US for the next month. I think he has to take a short trip to Sweden."

"So, what do you think?"

"I'd never rent it. To me it's like a golden prison. And I sure hope, when I retire, I don't end up like him. I'd be so bored."

"I suspect, at least I hope, you'll be doing more productive and less lascivious things in your retirement."

"I met another old guy on the beach, from Germany I think. He's a big hero here because he knows things like a small cookie on the beach should only cost ten pesos and tourists who don't know pay twenty pesos. He's a hero here, but he wouldn't be admired for anything if he returned to his country."

Nels heard the beeping of the motoconcho arriving and knew it was time to go. "Listen buddy, have a good night. And be safe. Novelee is here. I have to go."

Jonas said goodbye and Nels hung up the phone.

It was time for an adventure of his own.

Chapter Thirty-Eight

10:56 pm, Friday the 13th, Nels' apartment, Costambar.

Nels and Novelee had just finished making love. The experience wasn't all that bad, he had to admit, other than the dialogue during foreplay. Novelee had tried to convince Nels to make love to her without a condom, insisting that doctors had said she was unable to have children. When he had refused, she said he thought she was a liar. His out had been that perhaps the doctors had been wrong. He had seen it happen before. It seemed to satisfy her and they completed the session enjoyably and without any further drama.

They sat on the balcony. Novelee ate a ham and cheese sandwich, while Nels indulged himself in another rum punch.

Lately Nels had taken to stocking the fridge with a few easily prepared snacks so if Novelee got hungry-which she often did-then they wouldn't have to go out to a restaurant.

When he had first arrived, she had cooked him a few meals-mainly chicken, rice and beans and on a few occasions, pork chops or sausage, rice and beans.

But that had only lasted the first week-and lately she had no interest in cooking or cleaning-something she had done a lot of on his previous visits to the DR.

"Do you have any beer?" she asked Nels, finishing her sandwich. She had told him on three separate occasions she wasn't going to drink anymore. With her thyroid condition, her doctor had advised against it for the most part-excepting maybe the odd beer or two now and again.

"Sure," Nels said. He went into the kitchen and returned a minute later with a large Bohemia and a glass. He filled her glass and she took a sip.

"How's Jonas?" she asked.

"He's in Sosua right now."

"He likes that place, doesn't he?"

"He seems to."

"He's a very intelligent man."

"I agree."

There was a moment's pause before she continued.

"You know I'd still like to get my manicure salon set up. I figure it would cost about 10,000 pesos to buy everything I need."

Nels knew Novelee was very good at doing hands and feet, but he was done giving her large sums of money. He simply nodded and took a sip of his rum punch.

She poured herself some more beer and continued. "I didn't want to tell you this earlier but I thought you should know. Your friend Jonas might be a nice guy, but he tried to hit on me New Year's Eve."

"He did?" Nels asked, his eyebrows raised.

"Yes. I was talking to him about my plans to open a manicure salon, how much it would cost and everything. He told me if I was with him-as his girlfriend-he would send me the money. He gave me his phone number you know."

"He did?" Nels asked. He didn't believe the story and tried to figure out her motive for telling it. Money, he concluded, or a jealousy game.

"Yes, he did. But I tore it up, so you know. I'm not interested in him in that way. A lot of guys hit on me all the time and I always tell them I have a boyfriend."

It's funny how people's judgement can get extremely skewed after spending a few weeks, or a month, in an alcohol-induced state in the DR. And Nels' judgement was starting to become skewed, if it hadn't been a week after he arrived. But, in a rare moment of lucidity, he knew her story was a lie.

"Whatever you do, don't say anything to Jonas," Novelee said. "I don't want any trouble between you and your friend."

"Don't worry I won't," Nels said, not sure what he was going to do.

There was a long, uncomfortable silence. Nels drank his punch and Novelee sipped her beer. Occasionally, they would glance at one another.

"Say something to me," Novelee finally said.

"If you want me to say something, ask me a question," he said.

"Say something," she said again.

"Ask me a question," he said.

Another uncomfortable silence followed.

"I don't think you really love me," Novelee said.

Nels thought maybe she was right. He didn't know anymore. He rose from his chair, bent down and kissed her, long and full on the lips. He had to admit, she looked stunning in the light of the full moon. "Of course I love you honey. You're gorgeous. How could I not love you?"

She smiled at the response, seemingly satisfied.

He walked into the living room, flicked the TV on, knowing it would be a good diversion. His stomach suddenly felt upset and he wondered what he might have eaten to cause it.

Novelee had positioned herself on the couch, watching a movie.

"I'm going to bed," he said. "I don't feel well."

Nels walked into the kitchen, opened the fridge and poured himself a glass of water. He brought it into the bedroom, pulled out two Sedoxil pills, swallowing them with water.

Lying in the bed, he moved his hand under the mattress, located the handgun and gripped it tightly. He had found a new hiding place for his money belt.

Chapter Thirty-Nine

9:36 am, Saturday, January 14th, countryside, a few minutes from Puerto Plata, DR.

A bullet ricocheted off the rear bumper of the tan Trailblazer as Nels sped along the dusty road.

He was being chased by a black SUV and the driver was firing at him.

He reached into the glove compartment for the handgun. It wasn't there .*Shit!*

Another bullet cracked through the rear window, showering him with shards of glass. He accelerated, even though he could see a hair-pin corner ahead.

What choice did he have?

The vehicle careened onto two wheels as it rounded the corner and another bullet zinged passed him. He felt his hip pocket, looking for his cell phone. *Good!* It was in its familiar place. He slowed, navigating the Trailblazer back onto two wheels. It bounced, but then the tires found traction and rolled forward.

He found Juan's number and made the call. It rang four times before going to voice mail and he hung up.

Fuck, where are you brother?

He flashed a glance in the rear-view mirror. The black SUV was gaining on him rapidly.

Suddenly, it was right behind him. It smashed into his bumper, pushing his vehicle into a fishtail.

He tried to correct the skid, but he was going too fast and the SUV drifted sideways. The black SUV crashed into the driver's door, sending his SUV flying in the air. It flipped over, crunching-once-twice-three times before it skidded to a stop, the screeching sound of metal grating on gravel.

Nels was disoriented, but was finally able to roll down the window and slide his ass onto the road. He tried to stand up but a masked man kicked him in the jaw and he soared through the air, landing hard on his back.

He tried to roll over, get up and run, but the man's big black boot stomped on his chest, pinning him to the ground.

Knowing he was going to die, he tried to scream. Nothing came out.

The man pulled out a handgun and shot him twice in the head-pop-pop. He felt the life draining from his body, blackness enveloping him.

He suddenly jerked up in bed soaked with sweat, his heart pounding. Instinctively, he reached for the gun. He felt the cold comfort of steel.

He slowly got up, walked into the bathroom and splashed cold water on his face. He towel dried himself, his hands trembling from the nightmare, and looked at his image in the mirror. His short-cropped brown hair, was matted to one side, his green eyes bulged in their sockets.

He noticed for the first time dark circles forming under both eyes. His friends had always told him he looked much younger than his forty three years, but on this morning Nels thought the reflection in the mirror could easily be a man of fifty or better.

Shit, he thought. *So much for my youthful good looks.* He walked back into the bedroom, grabbed his eyeglasses from the bedside table and walked into the living room, looking for Novelee.

A note on the kitchen table said she had been called into work and wanted him to call later. It ended with the words, 'I love you.'

Nels walked into the kitchen, poured a glass of water and drained it, still thinking of the nightmare. He remembered having one other nightmare in his entire life in which he had died.

And, like this one, it had scared the living shit out of him.

He noticed his phone beeping and picked it up. It was a text message that read, 'Third one showing up soon. I named her Thulsa Doom.' It had evidently come from a blocked number.

"I have to get the fuck out of here," he said to himself.

Chapter Forty

1:36 pm, Saturday, January 14th, El Farolito Restaurant and Bar, beachfront, Costambar.

Nels sat drinking beer with Jonas and Ace, a Dominican friend whom Jonas had invited to Costambar for a visit.

Jonas had, at least for now, finished with his Sosewer sexcapades and had decided to return to Costambar for a few days. He had also completed some volunteer work, building homes for the poverty-stricken.

Nels had called him in the morning, informing him he had changed his plane ticket-he would be leaving for Canada tomorrow at 3:00 pm. He couldn't shake the impending feeling of doom, and wanted out of the DR as soon as possible.

Juan had stopped by for a quick visit a few minutes before he departed for the beach. Juan said he couldn't find any real dirt on Novelee, other than she had served a couple of short stints in the joint for assault causing bodily harm. Two of these stints were related to the pounding of her sister and a third, that went back about five years, was related to a knife attack on an Italian boyfriend. Apparently his arm had been slashed in the altercation.

For that incident, she had served two months in jail. From what information he could gather, the Italian had a history of violence and had apparently beaten Novelee on a few occasions. Her story, according to the court documents Juan had reviewed, had been a case of self-defense.

He couldn't find any evidence that would point to her operating within a gang, or with other associates.

"Ace protects foreigners," Jonas said in Spanish. "I met him about four years ago in the disco in Sosua. He's gotten me out of a few binds. He's one of the few Dominicans I've met who I trust completely."

Ace smiled at Nels, a winning smile. He was about five foot two, but extremely muscular for his size. His demeanor was easy going and happy and he cracked a lot of jokes and laughed a lot. His smart brown eyes instinctively scanned the sparsely populated beach. He ran his hands through his thick black long hair and sipped his Bohemia.

"I've done time in jail for protecting foreigners," Ace said. "There are a lot of bad people in my country and a lot of foreigners have no idea of the danger here."

"I'm glad there are people like you around here," Nels said, instantly liking Ace.

"One time," Ace said, "I was out at a bar in Puerto Plata and I saw an American friend being lured into a trap by a Dominican woman and a man who sat nearby, waiting for the right time to get involved. I recognized the people as scum, so I went over and threatened the woman. By that time her cohort had come over, started raising his voice to me. I told them in no uncertain terms to leave, but they wouldn't."

"So what did you do?" Nels asked. Jonas had heard the story before and only halfway listened as he stared at the ocean.

"I cracked him over the head with a beer bottle," Ace said.

"Did they leave?" Jonas asked.

"Oh yeah," Ace said smiling. Nels could tell this man had a dark side-but a dark side that was dedicated to upholding justice.

"Another time," Ace said, "I saw a tourist being held at knifepoint by a Dominican and robbed in broad daylight on the Malecon."

"What did you do?" Nels asked.

"I ran over, yelling at him to get lost, but he wouldn't listen. I got into a knife fight with him and he ended up with a large gash across his chest. Believe it or not I served time in jail for that."

Nels wasn't surprised. He knew at times the justice system in the DR didn't serve justice. He also knew you could bribe your way out of almost any problem-probably even murder.

"He's a straight shooter," Jonas said, smiling and holding up his glass. "To trustworthy Dominicans."

They clinked glasses and drank.

Nels' phone rang. It was Novelee. He had called her earlier in the day, explaining that job demands had forced him to change his flight itinerary-meaning today was his last day.

She had told him she would leave work early and meet him at his apartment at three in the afternoon. Her voice carried little emotion. He agreed and hung up the phone.

Nels had planned to visit his friends, owners of MarLou's Restaurant, later that evening-and he was hoping to send Novelee home before he went out-they had heard some of her history and indicated that yes, if she was with Nels, she was welcome at the restaurant-except leave the guns and knives at the door-please and thank you.

It was karaoke night at MarLou's and some of Nels' friends were planning a little send-off party.

He thought about mentioning Novelee's accusation to Jonas, but changed his mind. He still didn't believe the story but he would just like to get an opinion from Jonas. Perhaps some time in the future when his emotions didn't feel so raw.

He had thought about not answering his phone at all when Novelee had called. But if he had to be completely honest with himself, he still had some feelings for her.

And he also knew the little general was still commanding the troops-and he would not be denied one last night of carnal pleasure.

Chapter Forty-One

5:30 pm, Saturday, January 14th, Nels' apartment, Costambar.

Nels and Novelee had just finished making love-Novelee had performed dutifully, if not passionately.

They sat on the balcony- lounge chairs positioned opposite one another-sipping their drinks. Novelee drank a Bohemia and Nels sipped a Cuba libre.

Nels had spoken to Juan earlier, telling him he would Skype call when Novelee was ready to go. Juan had offered to drive her to her cousin's apartment.

Nels couldn't contain the happiness he was feeling at his departure tomorrow. He sang, "I'm leaving on a jet plane...and I'll never be coming back to you again."

Novelee glanced at him, puzzled. Otherwise, her face showed little emotion.

Nels smiled at her. He would not be denied his happiness. The dysthymia he had felt earlier in the day had all but vanished and the Dominican fog was rolling in-enveloping him with a comfortably numb feeling.

A few minutes later, her features darkened and she started questioning Nels.

"When you leave tomorrow, I'm leaving for the Semana peninsula. I have a job offer to work as a waitress in a new hotel. Will you visit me in there when you return?"

"Yes, I will," Nels said. "I've been to Semana before and it would be a nice change from Costambar. I think you mentioned it to me before."

Novelee eyed him curiously, trying to gauge his level of sincerity.

"When will you be coming back?" she asked.

"I have a lot of work to do," Nels said. "And I have an idea for a book I want to write. So, I'm not sure."

"I'm looking forward to leaving Puerto Plata," she said. "So many bad things have been happening to me lately and I want a fresh start. I just think I need more money to get to Semana."

Nels knew it wouldn't be long before the conversation shifted to dollars and cents. She wasn't outright asking, but she was hinting, as she often did. He didn't want to rock the boat-not now anyway. "I'll give you some money before I leave."

She smiled, her face lighting up-a picture of beauty and sincerity.

He thought he would start his story with a little money. He walked into the bedroom, retrieved a 500 peso note, brought it out and handed it to her.

She smiled and took it, without saying thanks. He didn't bother to remind her. "I'll give you some more later," he said.

After a moment's pause, he asked, "How are you feeling?"

"I have a slight headache, and I may have to work tomorrow."

It was the opening he was looking for. "My flight leaves very early tomorrow-six in the morning- so maybe we should hang out for a few more hours, then I'll give you some more money and have Juan drive you home. That way, you can be well rested before you go to work."

He was expecting some sort of story about it being his last night in town and she wanted to be with him, blah, blah, blah-but it didn't come.

"Okay," she said, deadpan.

An hour later, they were in bed again making love-she once more performed dutifully and without passion.

A few hours later, Nels sat in the front passenger seat alongside Juan as he steered the white Toyata Pathfinder into the ghetto, obeying Novelee's directions.

Novelee remained expressionless during the trip-Nels noticed none of the crying he had experienced during previous visits when he departed. On his last trip, she had become depressed for about a week prior to his departure-and, seeing him off at the airport, had not been able to contain her tears.

Nels didn't know if it had been his rejection of her earlier in the course of this trip-when he had blown her off for a few days- or the fact his patience level with everything was wearing thin, but things had obviously changed-for both of them.

That is, if he was willing to believe that she had ever really loved him. And, that was a conundrum he did not have an answer for. He remembered first meeting her at a Sosua disco, known infamously as hooker territory, a few years back. He had been partying with Jonas in the disco when Novelee had approached him with a girlfriend of hers-Dania he believed the name was-and started a conversation.

Nels and Jonas had been extremely drunk that night, drinking round after round of the famous Dominican cocktail, El Diablo. They had partied and danced until very late, before bringing both girls back to Nels' two bedroom apartment.

They had had a few more drinks at the apartment, before taking their respective partners into separate rooms to have sex.

The next morning, wrapped securely in the Dominican fog, they had left the apartment, first to stop at Jonas' apartment and then to take the women for lunch before calling a motoconcho to take them home to Puerto Plata.

Nels remembered Jonas walking five blocks in the opposite direction of where his apartment was located before finally getting his bearings.

They had eaten lunch on the beach, paid them each 1,000 pesos for their services, and sent them home.

Nels learned much later that Jonas had started a brief long distance relationship with Dania. But, it had only taken him about a month to figure out her agenda was all about money and he had ended it.

A few days after Jonas had departed, the frenetic pace of the Sewer had become too much for Nels and he had called his trusty cab driver Jose to rescue him. That's when he had relocated to Costambar and rented a one bedroom apartment at Tucan One.

During that time, Novelee had called Nels, relentlessly, about twelve times or more a day. He had followed his gut feeling about the woman for a few days-and when he had finally recovered from his drunken exploits in the Sewer, he had given in, answered the phone and invited her to meet him at El Farolito.

He remembered relaxing in a beach chair with a drink and watching her seductively stroll along the beach as she approached. He had thought to himself how much fun she would be in bed. Of course, the little general had taken over again.

She had sat down beside him and after a two minute conversation had told him she had fallen in love with him. It wasn't the first time he had heard it. She had also mentioned it on the phone.

"Right here, on the left," Novelee said, reaching for the three plastic bags of groceries she had acquired from Nels.

She had asked him about the groceries, insect repellent, other items, just before they had prepared to meet Juan poolside for the ride home. Nels had shrugged and said he wouldn't be needing them; so she had packed them up and brought them with her-of course, she didn't bother to thank Nels-and he didn't bother reminding her.

Nels hopped out of the car, opening the passenger door for Novelee. He reached in and grabbed a couple of the bags.

"I'll wait here," Juan said. "Don't be too long."

Nels nodded and walked with Novelee around to the back of the two story building. He passed about five doors, noticing a large pile of garbage in the backyard as they approached the door to her cousin's apartment.

She opened the door with her key. A small cute baby girl of about two years old looked up curiously at Nels. He set the bags down at the doorway, gave Novelee a quick kiss on the lips.

Novelee smiled and hoisted the small child into her arms. She kissed the baby. The baby giggled. So cute.

He asked the baby girl for a kiss. She looked at him beaming and pursed her little lips. Nels kissed her and she said, "I love you."

Although surprised, Nels said, "I love you too."

Before leaving, Nels glanced inside the apartment. A double bed, three chairs and a few dressers furnished the room and a door to a small bathroom was ajar. Novelee's cousin sat on the bed watching TV. Noticing Nels, she invited him in.

"No thanks," Nels said. "My friend is waiting. I have to go."

He looked at Novelee one last time, holding the small child and smiling. The child pursed her lips again, wanting another kiss.

He turned and walked away.

Chapter Forty-Two

12:36 pm, Sunday, January 15th, just outside the gates of Costambar.

Nels sat alongside Juan in the same white Pathfinder. Juan drove along the dirt road leading out to the main drag that would take them to the airport.

Juan had been teary-eyed when he knocked at Nels' door a few minutes earlier. He could tell his friend-no his brother-was going to miss him. Nels felt the same way. He admired Juan for his courage and sensitivity. He was a gentle giant, but also a warrior whom you would not want to cross.

After dropping Novelee off, they had arrived at MarLou's to a waiting group of about ten close friends, including Jonas. Nels made a point of becoming extremely drunk at the Karaoke night, at one point even getting up to sing John Denver's "Leaving On A Jet Plane" and Meat Loaf's "Paradise By The Dashboard Light."

They had partied until about 1:30 am, before Nels had decided to turn in. He wanted to be somewhat refreshed for the flights. He would have to take one plane to Newark, a connector to Ottawa for an overnighter, then a flight to Calgary the following morning, departing at 7:00 am.

Nels took a sip from his water bottle. It was half full with Brugal white rum-the other half water. He wanted to leave with a buzz.

They approached the intersection to the main drag, where they had to turn left. As they stopped, a black SUV suddenly slammed into the back of their vehicle, sending it zigzagging out into oncoming traffic. Cars and motoconchos sounded their horns, and a small red car that couldn't stop in time slammed into the driver's side rear quarter panel.

Juan didn't hesitate as one bullet whistled passed the vehicle and the other one smashed through the rear window, raining down broken glass and exiting through the windshield, a few inches from both of their heads. He jerked the steering wheel right, tossed his piece to Nels, saying "shoot" as he sped away.

Nels grabbed the handgun, turned around and fired two quick shots out the broken back window. One bullet blasted through the pursuing vehicle's windshield, while the other one missed completely.

"Don't worry," Juan said calmly as the high-speed chase began. "We'll get this motherfucker."

A minute later, they rounded a hairpin corner and Juan made a sharp left down a dirt road. The black SUV was right behind them.

It was déjà vu.

Nels' hands trembled holding the piece, flashbacks of his last nightmare playing on his muddled mind. *Will the dream come true? Is this it for me?*

Suddenly the black SUV was beside them. The driver fired two bullets, one of them piercing into metal on the lower door and the other slicing into Juan's left shoulder. Blood sprayed across his face and little droplets splashed onto the windshield.

Juan winced but remained calm. "Give me that gun," he said.

Nels handed it to him. Juan shot at the front tire of the black SUV, blew it out with a whooshing sound and it began spinning out of control. Juan slowed, the vehicle passed in front of him and he rammed the driver's side door just as it skidded sideways.

The driver grunted in pain on impact as Juan slowed, watching it flip end over end-one-two-three times before finally coming to a grinding halt upside down.

Juan stopped about twenty five feet behind the vehicle, jumped out the door, crouched down, leveled his gun and fired two quick shots-both of them penetrating the side of the man's head.

Nels got out and Juan motioned for him to stay back. Nels stood behind the Pathfinder and Juan approached the vehicle, gun drawn.

Juan looked down at the dead man, blood spurting from the fatal headshots.

For good measure, he shot him two more times in the head, before returning to the Pathfinder. Nels opened his small knapsack, ripped up one of his T-shirts, poured some of the rum and water mix into Juan's open wound and fashioned a tourniquet around Juan's shoulder with the shredded cloth.

Juan didn't wince when he poured the rum and water into the open wound. But he did take the bottle from Nels' hand and take a long drink from it.

Nels did the same when Juan handed it back to him.

"That should be all of them," Juan said, after making a quick call for a clean-up on aisle seven to one of his police connections.

"Who was he?" Nels asked.

"That's Fabiola's boyfriend Marcial," Juan said matter-of-factly. "He's the only one with any motivation to go after Fabiola's killer. And he certainly wouldn't go after Javier-so we were the next best thing. It's over now. You can relax."

"We need to get you to a hospital," Nels said.

"Don't worry. I'll deal with that later. You have a plane to catch."

Twenty minutes later, Nels stood outside the damaged Pathfinder, regarding his friend. Juan stood oblivious to the wound while his eyes welled up with tears.

"Remember, you are much more than a friend to me," he said, giving Nels a big bear hug. "You are my brother-you'll always be my little brother."

Chapter Forty-Three

3:36 pm., Saturday, January 21st, Nels' Woodlands house, Calgary, Alberta.

Nels pecked away at the keyboards of his laptop computer. He was three chapters into his first book. In many ways it would be a novel about Novelee. He had decided on the title: "Nightmare's Edge."

The first thing he had done after arriving home was call his psychologist aunt Julie. She had been his mentor starting at a very young age and had helped him exorcise many demons. He wanted to make some sense of all the nightmares. He had relayed a few of them to her, leaving out some of the drama.

"Nightmares have to be analyzed in the context of the upbringing of the person who is having them," she had said. "And yours was particularly troubling."

"What should I take from all this?" he had asked.

"Trust your nightmares," she had responded. "They're premonition dreams."

After he had hung up he thought about what she had said, before turning to an old file of story ideas he had started over twenty years ago. Flipping through it, he had noticed one of his nightmares scrawled on a tattered napkin.

He remembered it now. He had been trapped in a small dark prison cell in a foreign country and a beautiful woman had approached him wanting his company-and money. He remembered the nightmare being very sexual in nature, also remembered his friends warning him to stay away from her. But, in the end he had consummated the relationship sexually, had also given her money. It seemed the nightmare had foretold his future.

My nightmares foretell the future. Trust them. Believe in them. Learn from them.

He looked out the window at the snowflakes drifting down-it was frigid, minus 26 degrees Celsius outside, but the cold weather was the farthest thing from his mind. He sat at his desk in his luxurious and well-equipped office. He had taken a few days to recover-but finally his head had cleared and he felt lucid, energetic and productive. And grateful to be among the living. He hadn't had a drink since his return and he was finally off the sleeping pills and sleeping well.

He had yet to have a single nightmare, although he doubted they were gone forever. *I might even embrace them.*

He saw a Skype call flash on his screen-it was Jonas, who was still in the DR.

He picked up his headset, clicked answer. He had been unable to connect with his friend since his arrival. "How are you?"

"I'm doing good. Getting ready to leave tomorrow. Juan's driving me to the airport."

The two had met only briefly, but prior to his departure, Nels had mentioned to Juan to keep an eye on Jonas. He had talked to Juan a few times on Skype since his return.

"That's good," Nels said.

"Yeah, we've actually been out a few times for drinks. He's a great guy."

"He is. He calls me little brother, Nels said. "How's his shoulder?"

"Healing. It's in a sling." There was a long pause. "There's something I need to tell you," Jonas finally said. "And it might be a little painful. Have you talked to Novelee since you've been back?"

"No," Nels said. "Why?"

"Well she came to the beach the other day with her sister, Esmerelda and met me at the Catamaran. So you know, I didn't invite her, but she probably knew I was still here. Anyway, they both show up and of course they're hungry, so I buy them dinner and drinks. I ask Novelee if she's heard from you and she tells me it's over between the two of you."

"I don't know if I was planning on calling her, but go on."

"One thing leads to another and after dinner we go back to my apartment. Novelee has all her pedicure stuff with her and starts giving me a pedicure. When she finishes, they both try and get me to go to Puerto Plata, to meet the parents. I'm having no part of it, so Esmerelda leaves and Novelee and I party for a few hours, eventually ending up at MarLou's, where we run into Juan and Oria."

Nels breathed deeply. "What happened then?"

"Not much. We get drunk, of course Novelee gets hungry at about 1:30 in the morning so Juan drives us to a small chicken stand in Puerto Plata. Novelee takes one bite and then she decides she isn't hungry anymore. Anyway, she disappears into this dingy bar next to the chicken stand, comes out a few minutes later and asks me to join her. That's when Juan grabs me by the arm and tells me in no uncertain terms not to go inside that bar."

"Yeah. Keep going."

"Eventually, I get Juan to drive her back to her cousin's apartment in Puerto Plata. We drop her off, Juan drives me home and I crash out."

In spite of all the warnings Nels had received he couldn't help feel sad that Novelee would stray so quickly. "Well we never discussed our relationship was over, but it seemed to me the writing was on the wall. Be extremely careful with that woman. Underneath that innocent look is a violent and scheming person whose primary motivation is money."

"I never even considered doing anything with her," Jonas said. "But I wanted to warn you that I was right about her from the beginning. I just didn't know how to tell you earlier-you seemed to be in love with her. But, I want you to know, she was kind of hitting on me a little. I only entertained her so I could see her true colors-to warn you."

Nels inhaled deeply. "Anything else?"

"Yeah, there is. I didn't know how to say this to you before, but you remember New Year's Eve?"

"Yes."

"Well, she tried to get my phone number, wanted to come to Sosua to give me a pedicure and wanted to give me a hug, while we were having dinner. Of course, I would have none of it and told her so."

A long pause.

"Novelee told me, a few weeks back, and I never believed her for a minute, that you gave her your number, offered to give her money for her manicure salon idea if she left me and hooked up with you."

"That's a fucking lie," Jonas said, the agitation in his voice clear.

"Not to worry my friend. I think it's a case of one meal ticket leaves, and another potential meal ticket is still there," Nels said, realizing the Semana story was probably only one of her many lies.

The conversation shifted to the netbook, the missing money. After some discussion, Jonas said, "I think she did take the netbook and the money. When I think about it you still had the netbook after Fabiola left, and we gave Novelee way to much trust."

"I agree with you," Nels said. "Do you think I should tell Juan about it? He would ban her from Costambar and her reputation would be trashed in the area."

"I think you should," Jonas said. "She brought it on herself. And if we prevent one more unsuspecting tourist from being lured into her trap, we've done a good thing."

"I will tell him," Nels said.

"There's another thing I want to say," Jonas said. "I'm very sorry about what happened to you and, so you know, I used to consider myself a seasoned traveler. But, I find whenever I think that way down here that's when bad things happen to me-when I let my guard down. Anyway, the same thing happened to me a few years back. I thought I was in love. I went through lots of money and a one year relationship before I finally figured out the woman's primary motivation was money. It was painful."

"I think we can both learn, or relearn some of the things we thought we knew," Nels said.

"I agree," Jonas said. After some small talk, they ended their conversation-on a good note.

Nels Skype called Juan and got him on the line instantly. After some talk about Juan's health and the weather, Nels got to the point.

"So you know, Novelee is history," Nels said. He explained the missing netbook and money, pointing to Novelee as the most likely culprit.

There was a long silence before Juan finally answered. "This makes me feel uncomfortable. Why didn't you tell me before?"

I guess I wanted to believe her," Nels said. "And if I told you, you would have thought me crazy for still being with her, possibly even banned her from the building."

There was another long silence before Juan responded. "I warned you about her little brother. She's no good for you. And I never had a good feeling about her from the beginning."

"I'm just curious if she said anything to you when you saw her with Jonas?"

"Yes, she said everything is fine between you and her, but she also told me not to say anything to you, about her being out with Jonas. She said she didn't want you to get the wrong impression. But, don't worry. As I said to you, you need someone who is intelligent and has a job-someone more your equal. You're young and successful in your own right. You don't need a woman like that."

Nels digested the lies and frowned.

"She will never again be allowed past the gates of Costambar," Juan assured him.

A few minutes later they said their goodbyes.

In some ways he felt sorry for Novelee. Her pursuit of foreigners to extract money was in many ways a struggle for survival-a struggle for her next meal. But he doubted her low level mentality, the result of growing up poor, would ever change.

He doubted she would ever evolve from her current way of processing information.

But, he knew one thing. She was a scheming liar, probably a thief, had a violent temper and was willing and able to inflict physical violence to make her point. In his view, she was also an ill-tempered and ill-mannered negative thinker who viewed the glass as half empty.

There were serious trust issues here. And, without trust, what did you have?

He would probably never again call Novelee for the rest of his life. And he would try and remember the good times he had had with her. Maybe it was only his perception, but he felt she was a much better person only a year ago. And, he liked to believe, that she had actually loved him.

But he would never really know.

He had once thought of himself as a seasoned traveler. Now, he felt like a sucker.

But that chapter of his life was over now. But in *Nightmare's Edge* it was only beginning. At least writing the book will be good therapy, he thought, wondering if he would ever return to the DR.

But then it dawned on him. For all its craziness and quirkiness, there was a part of him that had become attached to the beauty of the country, to the good friends he had made on the little island. There was something about the DR, perhaps the lawlessness and adventure, that got into your blood. There, you felt like you were really living.

Sure, there were bad Dominicans. But, there were also many good ones.

He also felt changed from the experience, no longer taking anything for granted, enjoying life in Calgary-a city he had just over a month ago found so boring.

He had learned some important lessons in life: cherish and cultivate your friendships, find someone to love, follow your passion, and live every day as if it were your last day on earth.

He grinned, returning to his keyboard.

I know how it'll end.

Also by William Blackwell

Phantom Rage, Poison Rage, Infected Rage
Nightmare's Edge
Resurrection Point
Brainstorm
A Head for an Eye
Rule 14
Blood Curse
Black Dawn
Assaulted Souls
Assaulted Souls II
Assaulted Souls III
The Strap
The End is Nigh
Orgon Conclusion
Freaky Franky
The Witch's Tombstone
The Dark Menace
In Your Dreams
Macabre Alley
Tales of Damnation

The Strap Preview

"I loved this story, the plot was fast-paced but not too quick, the characters blend together really well especially Gray and Derrick. There's plenty of tension, suspense and action to keep you flying through the pages... I really enjoyed it and will be recommending it to my blogger friends." -Amazon

When Gray Eagleson remembers the strap, it brings back horrific images of pain, suffering and humiliation in the public school system.

Emotionally and financially strapped, he decides a trip to Ecuador is exactly what he needs for a fresh start. Before departing, he connects with Adriana Enrique on an internet dating site, promising to meet her on his arrival. He also helps his best friend Derrick Richmond evict some biker tenants involved in a marijuana grow-operation in one of Derrick's rental properties. One of the bikers, Stuart Treblecoch, aka The Strap, threatens to kill Gray for tossing biker belongings into a blazing backyard inferno.

Arriving in Ecuador, Gray soon discovers the idyllic vacation has turned into a life-and-death struggle. Adriana's erratic behavior casts a black shadow of doubt over his optimistic expectations, and he is terrified to learn The Strap is hunting him down. As the tension and violence ratchet up, Gray believes the mind-altering and spiritually enlightening drug ayahuasca is his only hope for salvation.

A taut psychological thriller, *The Strap* ushers you full-throttle deep inside the exotic sights and sounds of Ecuador while also exposing the very real dangers that exist. Through Gray's harrowing journey for personal redemption and survival, we discover the frailties and insecurities of the human condition and the ever-present need for companionship at the heart of human nature.

About the Author

Canadian dark fiction author William Blackwell studied journalism at Mount Royal University and English literature at The University of British Columbia. He worked as a journalist and a newspaper editor for many years before pursuing his passion for storytelling. His novels have been characterized as graphic, edgy, and at times terrifying. Currently living on a secluded acreage on Prince Edward Island, Blackwell finds much of his inspiration from Mother Nature, odd people, traveling, and bizarre nightmares.

Author Comments

Thank you for reading this book. I would be eternally grateful if you would post a book review on your favorite book retailer website. A positive review is the highest compliment a writer can receive. Reviews are crucial to the success of any author and they help readers discover new books. You don't have to say much. A few sentences will suffice.

In other news, I have a gift for you. Complete the signup form below with your name and email address and download a FREE copy of *Resurrection Point*, a dark tale about the horrifying consequences of experimenting with death and resurrection. You're only agreeing to be kept up to date on blog posts, new releases, and freebies. I promise I won't spam you and you can unsubscribe at any time.

Thanks again for your support.

http://www.wblackwell.com/free-ebook/